MONSTER SWAP

MONSTER SWAP

Robbie and Voxy
Zainab and Mash

Coming soon
Eddie and Fenda

MONSTER SWAP

Zainab and Mash

Written by
JONNY ZUCKER

Illustrated by
TONY ROSS

Hodder
Children's
Books

A division of Hachette Children's Books

To the stupendous Chris Witham and all of the wonderful staff
and pupils at Rhodes Avenue Primary School.

Text copyright © 2011 Jonny Zucker
Illustrations copyright © 2011 Tony Ross

First published in Great Britain in 2011
by Hodder Children's Books

2

A Catalogue record for this book is
available from the British Library

ISBN: 978 0 340 99711 6

Book design by Janette Revill
Printed and bound by CPI Group (UK) Ltd, Croydon, CR0 4YY

The paper and board used in this paperback by Hodder Children's
Books are natural recyclable products made from wood grown in
sustainable forests. The manufacturing processes conform to the
environmental regulations of the country of origin.

Hodder Children's Books
A division of Hachette Children's Books
338 Euston Road, London NW1 3BH
An Hachette UK company
www.hachette.co.uk

CONTENTS

After thousands of years spent hidden from human eyes, the earth's monsters have finally revealed themselves. From the murkiest swamps to the deepest forests, the monsters have emerged.

At first, humans were frightened of monsters. After all, seeing a giant purple two-headed monster dribbling mucus through your kitchen window would be enough to put any human off their cornflakes.

And at first, monsters were frightened of humans too. After all, seeing a tiny red-faced toddler human screaming for ice cream would be enough to put any monster off their sour cabbage and soil burgers.

So monsters set up the MONSTER COUNCIL FOR UNDERSTANDING HUMANS and humans set up the Human Agency for Understanding Monsters. Both organizations agreed that if monsters and humans were to stop being scared of each other they needed to find out as much as they could about each other's lives.

So they arranged a series of exchange visits. These 'Swaps' would involve a human child visiting a monster child in their monster world, followed by that same monster child visiting the human child in *their* world. No one had any idea how these visits would turn out ...

Welcome to the world of

ZAINAB
and the
OLYMPIC THIEF

Dear Coach Bulge
(Diploma in Belly Fighting and Mistress of Dribbling)

I'm writing to thank you for hosting the visit of Zainab Kaur – the human-monster exchange partner of Mash.

I've been told that Zainab's visit coincides with Mash's attendance at the Flamby Olympic Youth Trials. I understand the trials select which Flamby youngsters will represent your clan at the Northern Monster Olympic Games. It's very kind of you to let Zainab participate in these trials too. Although she is a talented athlete in the human world, her skills compared to a Flamby child might be lacking. If this is the case, I would appreciate it if you would refrain from repeatedly laughing in her face, or hitting her with a sharp pointed stick.

I should also warn you that Flambys have the tendency NOT to wait around for things like food and taxis, as you humans do. In fact, they take great pleasure in whacking each other out of the way. As a result of this, I expect Zainab's pushing and shoving skills will be much improved when she returns to the human world!

Wishing you every success with Zainab's visit.

Yours sincerely

Lady Bug Gazap

MONSTER COUNCIL FOR UNDERSTANDING HUMANS

1

Zainab Kaur shivered in the evening breeze and looked around in the dim light. A driver from the *Human Agency for Understanding Monsters* had just dropped her off on a long, twisting pathway covered in overgrown brown plants. Small silver bushes shaped like forks were dotted on either side of the path. They seemed to be talking to each other and giggling in shrill whispers. Zainab got the feeling they were laughing at *her*. Several narrow yellow volcanoes stood in the distance, puffing out large clouds of black smoke which rose into the air and then popped noisily. A series of mini-pools with frothing water were dotted over the landscape.

'Someone from the Flamby Olympic Trials will come to fetch you soon,' the driver had told her.

But there was no one in sight.

As Zainab was trying to decide what to do next she suddenly heard rustling in the bushes behind her.

She spun round.

Two points of red light flashed menacingly in the gloom and began advancing towards her. She gulped in terror and took a few hasty steps backwards. The lights edged closer to her.

'ZAINAB?' said a voice.

'Y ... y ... yes,' she answered.

'IT'S ME ... MASH!'

A Flamby monster emerged from the bushes. The thin red pulses were coming from the centre of his eyes and as he reached her she was covered in a halo of red light.

'MASH!' cried Zainab, relief pouring off her. 'Great to meet you!'

However much she'd prepared for this moment she couldn't stop herself gaping at the creature in front of her. He was six feet tall with purple, bumpy skin. On either side of his head were three diamond-shaped ears sprouting thick purple hair. His short trunk had six openings at its end. His thick arms had very tiny hands with three small fingers, and two long wavy legs ended in seven sausage-like toes. A single strand of hair jutted up on top of his head.

'Great to meet you too!' laughed Mash, slapping her in the face.

'HEY!' cried Zainab, her cheek stinging with pain. 'What was that for?'

'It's the traditional Flamby greeting,' explained Mash. 'You have to do it to back to me.'

Zainab paused for a second and then whacked him in the face.

'Excellent!' beamed Mash. 'Now we've said hello, let's get going.'

They turned right and headed up the pathway. Several of the fork bushes followed them at a slight distance, whispering and chuckling amongst themselves.

'So how do these Olympic trials work?' asked Zainab, who had to jog to keep up with Mash's long strides.

'All Flamby kids compete in regional heats,' explained Mash. 'The eight of us who won those heats were invited for proper trials here. Anyone who wins an event in this place gets a gold medal *and* joins the real Flamby team for the Northern Monster Olympics!'

'That sounds amazing!' marvelled Zainab. 'What kind of events will there be at these trials?'

'No idea!' cried Mash. 'They're brand-new each year so no one can practise! You're doing the events too, aren't you?'

Zainab nodded. She'd been picked for this particular swap because she was an excellent runner, gymnast, footballer and skateboarder.

Competing against these massive Flambys is going to be a tough challenge, thought Zainab.

They walked round several bends and then headed off the path towards one of the yellow volcanoes. Balancing very precariously on top of it was a huge structure made from bamboo shoots and bits of string. Lengths of bamboo jutted out in every direction, giving the building the appearance of a very oddly shaped skeleton. It seemed that all it would take to knock it from its perch would be a small gust of wind.

'The Flamby Olympic Centre of Excellence, at the top of Tuft Volcano!' declared Mash proudly, pointing to the structure.

'What, we're staying up *there*?' gulped Zainab.

'Don't worry,' smiled Mash. 'It's never fallen down – at least not yet!'

'But what if Tuft Volcano erupts?' asked Zainab.

'It never has,' replied Mash, 'at least not yet!'

Carved into the side of the volcano was a set of steep steps. They climbed these until they reached the top, where they found themselves standing in front of a wide bamboo door leading inside the building. Mash gave the door a kick and it crashed open.

They went inside and found themselves in a long corridor. The floor was covered in some kind of bouncy checked material. There were doors on both sides of the corridor and Zainab spotted a sign at the far end saying: **CANTEEN THIS WAY**. To their right was a flight of wonky bamboo steps.

'I got here about an hour ago,' said Mash, bouncing over the springy floor. 'All of the other contestants were already asleep, but I still managed to grab us a room with really fast beds!'

Fast beds? thought Zainab. *What does he mean?*

Mash bounded towards the steps and started jumping up them. As Zainab climbed up after him, she gazed at the pictures of Flamby Olympic heroes from the past, which were displayed on the walls of the stairwell. She was particularly impressed by a female Flamby called Doozy Flinka who had won the Porcupig Chase six years in a row. The single hair on Doozy's head had been twisted to make it resemble an arrow.

Zainab ran to catch up with Mash and at the top of the stairs they turned left, passing several closed doors on their right. Zainab noticed that every door in the building had a small purple box attached to it – which she assumed were doorbells – and a number. She and Mash stopped outside Room 83.

The door was open.

'This is us!' declared Mash.

Inside was a simple square space, with bamboo walls and a bamboo floor. On the floor were three long oval lengths of wood. Each of these was mounted on a circular metal base.

Those beds look spectacularly uncomfortable!

There was an opening in the room for a window but there was no glass. Apart from a small bamboo table, the only other thing in the room was a long empty shelf above the door. Mash's stuff was on the floor next to the bed nearest the 'window', so Zainab placed her bag down beside the bed next to it.

'I've got a great snack for us!' she grinned, pulling a gigantic chocolate bar out of her bag.

'What's that?' asked Mash.

'It's the sweetest, most delicious thing you'll EVER taste!' Zainab replied dreamily. 'But do you agree that we should only eat it at a midnight feast?'

'Absolutely!' yawned Mash. 'Midnight is the only time for grub. But it'll have to wait till tomorrow. I'm exhausted and midnight's not for ages. If we sleep well, we'll compete well. We'd better hide that chocolate thing. If Coach

Bulge sees it, she'll go crazy!'

Coach **Bulge**? *She sounds scary!*

Mash knelt down, took a quick look at the wall, and pulled a hidden section out of his trunk. It was a pair of pliers, and he used these to pull away a bamboo panel, revealing a small hole behind it.

'Perfect!' grinned Zainab, stashing the chocolate bar inside. Mash replaced the bamboo panel and flung himself on to the oval bed nearest the window. The second his body made contact with it, the bed started spinning round on the circular metal base, slowly at first, but quickly picking up speed.

Zainab stared in amazement at the rotating bed and its rotating passenger.

Gingerly she placed a foot on the bed next to Mash's. As soon as her toes touched it, the bed began to rotate.

She pulled her foot away and it stopped.

'Er … Mash,' she said softly.

Mash was now spinning at a fantastic pace and the whirring sound of his bed meant he couldn't hear her.

'MASH!' she shouted at the top of her voice.

Mash sat up and jumped off his bed, which immediately stopped rotating.

'What's up?' he asked.

'I don't think I'll be able to sleep on a spinning

bed,' said Zainab.

'Really?' he asked with surprise. 'You sleep without moving?'

Zainab nodded.

'OK,' he said, flicking a switch underneath the base of Zainab's bed. She put her foot back on it and it stayed perfectly still.

'Thanks, Mash!'

'No problem,' he grinned, leaping back on to his bed. In a minute he was spinning at great speed again.

Zainab laid her sleeping bag out on her bed and climbed inside. In spite of the draught coming through the no-glass window, and the wooden surface of the bed, it was actually pretty comfy and even though the whirring sound from Mash's bed was quite loud, it wasn't long before she fell into a deep and very much *non-spinning* sleep.

2

Zainab was woken by someone lifting her up in the air by her left ear. Her eyes snapped open and she came face-to-face with a huge female Flamby who had a whistle hanging off each of her ears.

'You must be Zainab,' stated the Flamby. 'I take it you arrived late last night?'

Zainab nodded.

'I'm Coach Bulge – Olympic trials organizer, referee and all-round head honcho.'

'Could you let go of my ear, please?'

Bulge let go and Zainab crashed to the floor.

'Welcome to the Flamby trials,' said Bulge in a business-like fashion. 'If you perform well at these events, I will strongly advise the human Olympic selectors to look out for you!'

'Really?' gasped Zainab. To compete in an Olympic games was her number one dream.

The Coach's gaze then fell on Mash, who was still whizzing round on his bed, deep in slumber. Bulge aimed a mighty kick at his backside, which sent him flying on to the floor.

'MASH, I PRESUME?' barked the Coach.

'Absolutely! Totally! Definitely!' said Mash, scrambling to his feet before saluting.

'Breakfast starts in five minutes and forty-seven seconds,' Bulge informed them, checking her very large aqua-blue watch. 'Do NOT be late!'

And with that she strode out of the room.

Five minutes and forty-six seconds later, Zainab and Mash hurried into the canteen. This was a long rectangular room with several holes in the ceiling to let in light and a large bamboo serving hatch at the far end, with its shutter closed. There were no tables, chairs or cutlery in sight.

ER ... where do we eat?

Coach Bulge was there, surrounded by six Flamby kids.

'Greetings, Zainab and Mash,' called the Coach. 'I'd like you to meet Rop, Flub, Kimban and Arg – our female Flamby competitors; and Crust and Yag – our males. Everyone – this is Mash and his human exchange pal, Zainab.'

The Flamby kids ran over to greet them with smiles, slaps and toe shakes.

'Don't you have any sprouts of ear hair?' enquired Flub, stroking Zainab's nose with the brush section of her trunk.

'They mostly don't have ear hair!' said Rop. Don't you ever watch *Humanville*?'

'I thought there were *eight* Flamby contestants?' said Mash, but before Coach Bulge could reply, a deep voice bellowed out, 'LET'S BE HAVING YOU!' as the serving hatch shutter was thrown open.

Everyone turned to see a huge Flamby with a skull and crossbones tattoo on his forehead and a pirate hat balancing in a lopsided fashion on his head.

'Good morning, Chef Cutlass,' declared Bulge.

'Morning, Admiral!' shot back Cutlass.

Chef Cutlass used to be a monster pirate cook, whispered Mash to Zainab. *'But when his ship was eaten by enemies he came to live on land. Now he's the official Flamby Olympic cook!'*

'Chef Cutlass will only be making and serving

24

healthy food during your stay here!' stated Bulge, looking round the room at the contestants. 'Neither of us will tolerate the eating of ANY foods that are sweet or sugary.'

'No sweets and no sugar!' growled Cutlass, eyeing the contestants with a fierce pirate-like stare.

'Have we made ourselves clear?' demanded Bulge.

Everyone nodded.

Zainab and Mash exchanged a guilty glance, thinking about the hidden chocolate bar in their room.

Cutlass began loading a stack of gooey brown shapes into the mouth of a large silver cylinder with a trigger on its underside.

'Why is Chef Cutlass holding a gun?' asked Zainab.

'It's not a gun, it's a Splatter,' explained Mash. 'He's loading it with Chunky Floop Pies!'

'ALL RIGHT, LANDLUBBERS!' cried

Cutlass, holding his Splatter up. 'GET YER GRUB NOW!'

He squeezed down hard on the Splatter's trigger and swept it from side to side across the room.

Immediately the Splatter started pumping out pies in all directions. The contestants and Coach Bulge began racing round the room, leaping through the air, and attacking each other as they tried to catch the pies in their mouths.

Zainab stood in complete shock for a few seconds until she realized that if she didn't join in SHE'D GET NOTHING TO EAT. So when she saw a pie heading her way, she lunged for it. Yag, however, had spotted it too. He skidded across the floor, tripped Zainab up and snatched it for himself.

OK, so you wanna play it like that!

Zainab leapt back to her feet and chased Yag, who was heading in the direction of another pie. As his trunk reached out for it, she shoved him on the back. He toppled over with a yelp. She jumped up, caught the pie and took a couple of quick bites. It tasted like hedgerow and burnt marmalade, but with Kimban now running towards her, she quickly polished it off, before scanning the canteen for another one.

In the next minute she was pushed aside by Coach Bulge, thrown on to the floor by Rop and whacked in the stomach by Flub. But by diving between Arg's legs she managed to snaffle another pie. This time she didn't bother chewing; she just swallowed it in one great gulp.

I don't think they'd allow this kind of eating in my school canteen!

A few moments later Coach Bulge blew a shrill note on one of her whistles and everyone stopped moving. By the smiles on everyone's faces, it seemed that a) they'd all managed to get something to eat, and b) there were no bad feelings about the mad fight to grab the pies.

Coach Bulge was about to make another announcement when a Flamby kid wearing a huge gold chain wrapped around his left ears ambled into the canteen. He was carrying a large bag made of knotted lengths of rope. He shot a haughty look round the room and sidled over to the counter.

'Fix me something to eat and make it snappy!' he barked at Chef Cutlass.

Cutlass raised himself to his full height and reached for his Splatter. 'No one, on land or at sea, has EVER talked to me that way!' he snarled.

'It's all right, Chef!' said Coach Bulge, hurrying across to the counter. 'This is Bib – our eighth Flamby contestant. He's obviously just arrived and has clearly forgotten his manners!'

'Where's my grub?' demanded Bib.

Bulge's eyes grew large with anger, but she managed to reply in a calm fashion. 'As you are late, all you get is leftovers.'

She stepped into the kitchen, grabbed some

discarded scraps of Chunky Floop Pies off the floor and shoved them into Bib's hands.

'You ... you ... expect me to eat this?' cried Bib.

But Coach Bulge ignored him and announced: 'We will now proceed to our introductory training session.'

Bulge led the contestants out of a door at the side of the canteen, and down the steep steps of Tuft Volcano. Bib was last and although he was tutting furiously, Zainab noticed he ate all of the Floop Pie off-cuts. Everyone followed Coach Bulge along a dusty, twisting path until they reached a large rectangular area that was covered in yellow goo from an erupting volcano just beside it.

'Right,' declared Coach. 'There will be no gold medals this morning, but I want everyone to work hard in these warm-ups as I will be watching you and assessing your abilities. First off I want thirty elbow press-ups.'

Zainab watched as the others fell on to the ground and began bouncing their bodies up and down with the use of just one elbow.

'Zainab, you may use the human press-up position,' called Coach.

Luckily, Zainab was fit, so thirty press-ups was no big deal.

Bulge then got everyone to do a series of stretches, turns and runs, followed by weight-lifting – where they lifted each other (Zainab did brilliantly to lift Mash a couple of centimetres off the ground), speed crawling and body rolling. This was followed by running, hopping and jumping great distances. A couple of times Zainab got her foot caught in a puddle of the sticky volcanic goo but a strong yank was all it needed to free herself.

During the activities, Bib kept on muttering things like, 'This is way too easy for me' and 'Boring!' although he did it quietly enough so that Coach Bulge couldn't hear.

When the session drew to a close, Chef Cutlass appeared, carrying his Splatter. This was filled to the brim with Nutty Floop Pancakes.

'Is *everything* round here made of Floop?' asked Zainab, hoping that maybe it wasn't.

'Of course!' replied Mash. 'But we cook it in so many different ways!'

Although the training session had been tiring, everyone still fought like crazy over the pancakes. As soon as they'd finished eating, Coach Bulge rubbed her hands together and declared in a loud, booming voice,

'IT IS NOW TIME FOR THE FIRST EVENT!'

The eight excited Flamby contestants and Zainab snaked down a long sandy path, past a huge fenced-off area with a gushing river running through it.

'I can't believe we're about to do a real event!' cried Mash. 'I SO want that first gold medal.'

Bulge and the contestants reached a large circular space with a smooth, shiny, dark blue surface. On this were a series of holes, walls, alleyways, slopes and ditches. These were all made out of bubbly, white foam material. Around the edges of the circle was short-cut light blue grass.

'It's a Flamby obstacle course!' said Mash.

I wish I'd brought my skateboard, thought Zainab. *It would be excellent here!*

'CONTESTANTS, INFLATE YOUR BELLIES, PLEASE,' ordered Bulge.

Zainab watched in astonishment as Mash and the Flambys pressed down on their grey belly buttons. She heard streams of whooshing air as their midriffs began to expand. Within a minute their stomachs had taken on the shape of half an inflated beach ball.

'Zainab, you can use this,' said Coach Bulge.

She handed over an athletic vest with Velcro straps on the front and a red semi-circular inflatable, also with Velcro straps. Zainab donned the vest and Bulge helped her attach the inflatable to her front.

'You may practise *outside* the circle!' declared Bulge.

The Flambys dived on to their fronts and

started bouncing around on the light blue grass. A wide grin spread across Zainab's face as she got the idea and flipped on to her stomach. At first, her bounces were too strong and she shot wildly into the air, hitting the ground with massive force. But after ten minutes of practice she felt much more in control. She could now turn, jump, speed up and slow down.

All of those bouncing workouts at trampoline club are paying off!

'That's enough practice!' bellowed Bulge. 'Take up your starting positions.'

The nine contestants bounced on to the shiny dark blue surface and arranged themselves behind the black starting line. Zainab was on the far left with Mash on her inside.

'I can win this, I know I can,' whispered Mash.

'The red arrows show you the route of the course,' explained Bulge. Zainab stared ahead at the arrows, her body tensed for the starting order. Bulge checked the contestants were all behind the line, then raised a whistle and blew.

Everyone crashed forward together, bouncing, barging and bellowing.

Zainab flew along the initial straight and then down the first slope. She managed to get her jump just right so that she cleared the low wall at the end. She bounced through a narrow passage and over a stile. She was near the back, just in front of Yag. Rop, who was just ahead of her, bounced too high over a stile and landed in one of the holes. As he struggled to free himself, Zainab overtook him.

This is WICKED! I'm a bouncing bomb!

She bounced up a ramp, catching up with Flub. Flub barged her but she managed to stay on course by swerving left. She looked up and saw Mash ahead. He was speeding round the course in second place just behind Kimban.

Go, Mash!

Zainab bounced over a ditch, neck and neck with Bib. Neither of their jumps was long enough to clear the murky water. Luckily Zainab hit a rock and bounced straight out. Bib wasn't so lucky; he smacked on to the water and paddled desperately while trying to lever himself out.

Zainab flew between some giant fixed skittles, coursed beneath three low arches and skidded round a tight bend. She was now in fourth place, just behind Crust. Up ahead, Mash had edged past Kimban into pole position.

You can do it, Mash!

The finish line was now in sight and Zainab gazed in awe as Mash took a tremendous bounce and went shooting further ahead of Kimban. But he got his angles wrong and instead of flying into a first-place finish, he smashed down into a crater and stuck fast. Kimban flipped on

to her feet and whizzed past him across the finish line, followed by Crust. As Zainab neared Mash, she grasped his trunk and with a mighty effort managed to drag him out of the crater. He slumped across the finish line in third with Zainab just behind in fourth.

'WELL DONE, KIMBAN!' beamed Coach Bulge, placing a dazzling gold medal round Kimban's neck. 'You have just earned yourself a place on Team Flamby for the Northern Monster Olympics!'

Most of the other contestants were generous in their praise for Kimban, with lots of trunk shakes and tugs of ear hair. Mash managed a 'well done' but he was clearly very disappointed in his performance and could hardly press his belly button to start the deflation process.

'You ran a good race, Mash,' said Coach Bulge, walking over to him. 'But you went for glory at the end and lost your focus.'

Mash said nothing.

'And *you* did very well,' nodded Bulge, patting Zainab on the shoulder, and helping her get out of the beachball/velcro outfit.

A soaking wet Bib stomped past them, spitting out murky water and muttering angrily.

'That was probably the event where I had the biggest chance of winning,' said Mash glumly after Bulge had gone off to talk to Flub.

'How can you say that!' cried Zainab. 'It was only the *first* one! We have no idea what the others will be.'

'But belly-bouncing is a speciality of mine. That race could have been *designed* for me.'

'Come on, Mash,' said Zainab brightly, 'I bet you're a brilliant all-round athlete. You're bound to win *one* of the gold medals.'

But as they walked back towards the Flamby Olympic Centre, Mash's long face showed he didn't, in any way, share Zainab's optimism.

4

It wasn't long before Zainab managed to talk Mash into a better mood, by telling him stories about Mr Armoury, her zany teacher back home. And Mash's spirits rose even further when they entered the canteen for supper and he saw Chef Cutlass loading some flat things into his Splatter.

'Floop Patties!' beamed Mash. 'My favourites!'

'HERE COME THE EATABLES!' cried Cutlass, squeezing the Splatter's trigger.

This time Zainab didn't wait to get stuck in; she instantly tripped up Crust and snaffled a patty he'd been reaching for. After the melee

and the patty-eating was over, everyone – apart
from Bib – stayed in the canteen, chatting about
the day's activities and what might happen
in the rest of the trials. It was very late when
Coach Bulge ordered them all upstairs.

'Tomorrow's a huge day!' she reminded them.
'So it's straight to bed!'

When Zainab and Mash returned to their
room, they found that all of their stuff had been
moved from the floor and chucked up on the
wonky shelf above the door. And furthermore,
Bib was asleep in Mash's bed.

'What's *he* doing in here?' snarled Mash.

'I don't know,' replied Zainab, 'but it's coming
up to midnight, so let's have the midnight feast
first and deal with him later.'

'Nice idea!' nodded Mash. He knelt down,
his pliers slid out of his trunk and he removed
the wall panel. But instead of pulling out the
chocolate bar, he swept his trunk about inside
the hole.

'I don't believe it!' he hissed.

'What?' said Zainab.

'It's gone!'

'It can't have!' responded Zainab, lying down on the floor and gazing into the space.

But Mash was right.

The chocolate bar was nowhere to be seen.

'I was SO looking forward to tasting it,' said Mash angrily. 'Not only has Bib taken my bed, he's also stolen the midnight feast!'

Mash stamped over to where Bib was sleeping and pressed the button on the underside of his bed. The bed came to a crunching halt and Bib was thrown off. He rolled over the floor and banged into the wall. Rubbing his bleary eyes, he looked up at first with confusion and then with fury at Zainab and Mash.

'WHAT DO YOU THINK YOU'RE PLAYING AT?' he demanded.

'FIRST YOU STEAL MY BED, NOW YOU NICK OUR GRUB!' thundered Mash.

Bib stood up. 'For your information, this was the only room with any space in it when I arrived here this morning,' he hissed. 'I didn't know you OWNED this particular bed. And as for your "grub", I have no idea what you're talking about!'

'It must be you!' fumed Zainab.

Mash smelt Bib's breath but there was no

aroma of any sweetness. He looked in Bib's bag and under the bed but there was no sign of any chocolate. He and Zainab checked every millimetre of the room, but again, no choc.

Mash was so frustrated and angry that he leapt into the air. Unfortunately he hit his head on the wonky shelf above the door and Zainab's bag came smashing down on his left foot.

'NOT MY LEFT FOOT FUNNY BONE!' shouted Mash as his left foot began frantically pounding up and down on the floor.

It took a good minute for his left foot to stop its crazed motions. During this time, Bib grabbed his stuff and stamped over to the bed nearest the door. 'You can have your stupid bed back,' he shouted, 'but DON'T BOTHER ME AGAIN!'

Within a minute his new bed was spinning at a mighty speed and he was fast asleep.

'He *must* have taken it,' seethed Mash. 'He was the only one in here.'

'But we have no proof!' sighed Zainab, looking round the room as if the chocolate might suddenly magically reappear.

After whispering to each other about the stolen chocolate for close to an hour, Zainab and Mash eventually got into their beds and fell asleep.

But it wasn't with a delicious sugary tang on their lips; it was with a very bitter taste in their mouths.

*

'Psst, Mash.'

Mash opened his eyes and pushed the button underneath his bed so it came to an abrupt stop. It was morning. Shafts of sunlight were streaming in through the non-window.

'I just got a jumper out of my bag and I found these,' whispered Zainab.

She held up a large pack of Caramel Marvels. 'I'd completely forgotten I packed them.'

'Brilliant! Let's eat them now!' grinned Mash.

'No!' said Zainab. 'We agreed to only eat sweet stuff at a *midnight feast*, remember?'

Mash looked disappointed but he nodded.

'I don't want to leave them in here with Bib around,' whispered Zainab.

'I know a much better hiding place than that wall gap,' replied Mash.

They slunk out of the room and hurried down to the end of the corridor. Mash pointed to a small square hatch in the ceiling. 'I think it leads to some kind of loft,' he whispered. 'I spotted it last night.'

Zainab nodded, climbed on to Mash's back and pushed open the hatch. Mash was right; it opened out into a small attic. Zainab pulled herself up and stood in the space. It was just about tall enough for her to stand in. It smelled of woodchips and sour milk. There were some old monster sports magazines stacked up on the floor and some kind of giant-sized monster goalkeeper gloves. Zainab placed the Caramel

Marvels down on a small broken bamboo table.

At that exact second she heard Coach Bulge nearby, shouting at everyone to get up. Zainab quickly started to lower herself out through the gap but the back of her shirt got caught on a nail in the hatch door.

At that instant Bulge strode round the corner and stopped.

'What are you up to?' she asked Mash, who looked both shocked and very guilty.

'Er ... just doing some early morning warm-ups,' replied Mash, jumping on to his front and doing some elbow press-ups at a furious pace.

Directly above Coach Bulge, Zainab swung from the hatch door.

Please don't look up!

'Hmmmm,' replied Bulge, eyeing Mash suspiciously. She was just about to look up when Kimban – who'd heard her voice – called from round the corner.

'Coach Bulge, have you got any toe juice?'

Bulge sighed, gave Mash another suspicious look and hurried off to see Kimban. The second she'd gone, Mash reached up and unhooked Zainab's shirt with the knitting needles section of his trunk. Zainab flicked the hatch shut and slid down Mash's back.

'That was SO close,' she said with relief.

'I know,' agreed Mash, 'but at least we know that no one will find the Caramel Marvels!'

'Too right!' grinned Zainab. 'Midnight feast here we come!'

When they got to the canteen for breakfast, Chef Cutlass was piling Floop crispbread into his Splatter. Zainab was now so used to the argy-bargy at mealtimes that she could hardly remember eating without a good fight first.

After Cutlass had fired and the battle had finished, Bib sidled up to them. 'How dare you wake me in the night and accuse me of stealing!' he hissed angrily.

'You were the only one there,' retorted Zainab.

'Well, you two losers shouldn't bother turning up to any events today,' said Bib with a sneer.

'And why is that?' enquired Zainab.

'Because I'll wipe the floor with everyone – especially you two!'

'You don't even know what the events are,' retorted Mash.

'I don't need to,' sneered Bib. 'I'm the best athlete here and my talent will shine through!'

'Yeah, yeah!' said Zainab dismissively. She was about to say more but there was suddenly a colossal crashing sound and a giant, salivating green beast smashed through one of the canteen walls and let out a

TERRIFYING ROAR.

The contestants screamed and raced for the exit as shards of bamboo showered over the canteen.

'STOP RIGHT THERE!' bellowed Coach Bulge.

Even though the contestants were terrified, they didn't want to disobey Coach Bulge and endanger their Monster Olympic chances, so they stopped and turned round to take a closer look at the beast.

Its dark green eyes were as large as truck wheels, green bile was dribbling from its gnashing mouth, and brownish wisps of smoke wafted out of its nostrils.

'This is my old friend Twang,' announced Coach Bulge, placing an arm round the beast's shoulder. 'He's from the Azoobi Monster Clan and he's going to be helping us out with a couple of the events here.'

'Why didn't you just come in through the door?' asked Mash.

'Why use a door when there's a wall nearer?' replied Twang with a cheeky grin.

'How can that dribbling creature be central to an Olympic trial?' demanded Bib.

'Never judge a monster by his dribble,' replied Coach Bulge, shooting Bib a filthy glare.

Bulge led the contestants out through the destroyed wall while Chef Cutlass began the job of patching it up.

Down the Tuft Volcano steps they proceeded and along a path that had been cut between two fields containing tall, spindly orange crops with giant orange and black flowers. They crossed a trickling scream and Zainab spotted a long reddish fish whose body seemed to go on for ever. A few minutes later they entered a rickety old barn, the walls of which seemed to have been made from chunks of junk metal. Here was a rusty car engine; there was a large, dented steel front door; here was a set of twisted hammers and screwdrivers. In front of the walls large blue bales of hay were haphazardly stacked.

'Gather round, please,' instructed Bulge.

Twang stood at her side, droplets of green goo sliding out of his mouth.

'I believe, Zainab, that at fairs in the human world you have an event called the Bucking Bronco?' said Coach Bulge.

'We do,' nodded Zainab. 'It's when you sit on a mechanical horse that moves really wildly and you try to stay on for as long as possible. In some places they use real horses.'

'Well, we're going to be using something

that's very real,' nodded Bulge, 'and he's called Twang. Though, in this case, instead of holding on to his *back* you will be holding on to his *belly*.'

Zainab and Mash looked on with fascination as Twang started pulling stringy black tentacles of different lengths and diameters out of his stomach.

'Do we get a practice go?' asked Yag hopefully.

'Absolutely not!' replied Bulge. 'I have drawn a random order and ... Flub, you're on first.'

'I really think I can win this one,' whispered Mash to Zainab. 'I went on something like this at my school jumble sale. I won a whole family of Geeboo fish.'

'What did you name them?'

'Nothing,' replied Mash, 'I ate them all.'

Flub stepped forward and inspected the black tentacles with a keen eye. She selected the two longest ones she could find and grabbed them with a tight grip.

'Twang, are you all set?' asked Coach Bulge, checking her stopwatch.

'TWANG IS READY!' dribbled the monster. Huge plumes of smoke were now billowing out of his nostrils.

'OK, Flub,' nodded Bulge, 'your time starts … NOW!'

Immediately, Twang sprang into action. He bounced, he shook, he twisted, he bumped, he kicked his hooves in the air. Flub crashed in all directions, hanging on with grim determination. But it wasn't long before she was hurled through the air, straight into one of the blue wheat bales.

'Fifteen seconds,' declared Coach Bulge. 'Next up is Yag.'

Yag went for thickness of tentacle as opposed to length, but only managed two seconds more than Flub.

Kimban did nineteen seconds; Arg managed nine; Rop did eleven.

'OK, Zainab,' nodded Bulge, 'you're on!'

Zainab swallowed nervously.

She walked up to Twang, shinned up on to his belly and grabbed hold of two of his shorter tentacles. Mash gave her an encouraging grin and mouthed, 'Go for it!'

'BEGIN!' shouted Bulge.

Zainab's stomach lurched and her body shook as Twang threw himself around like a crazed beast. The other contestants swam in a blur before her eyes; her bones jangled like beads on a wafer-thin necklace. But she used her experience from tug-of-war battles to hang in there for as long as possible and when she was finally flung off, Coach Bulge clapped her hands.

'Twenty-three seconds!' she declared delightedly. 'Our human contestant is in the LEAD!'

Everyone else clapped, apart from Bib, who scowled at her.

'It's your turn now, Mash,' declared Bulge.

Mash strode over to Twang, his jaw set in a steely pose. He climbed up Twang's belly and took a few moments to select three tentacles.

'Get on with it!' muttered Bib irritably.

'GO!' shouted Bulge.

Twang began to thrash around madly again. Mash was thrown left and right and up and down, but he hung on with grim determination and he was finally ejected in twenty-seven seconds.

'AMAZING!' grinned Zainab, when Mash walked over to her.

'Thanks,' said Mash with a modest smile.

Mash was in first place, Zainab was in second.

Not a bad position!

'It's now your turn, Bib,' declared Bulge.

Bib selected one thick tentacle and wrapped his body around it. This strategy seemed to work because by the time he was thrown off, he'd achieved a time of thirty-one seconds.

'I WIN!' bellowed Bib.

'Not so fast,' said Bulge, 'Crust hasn't had his turn yet.'

'Can't we just forget about Crust and cut to the part where I get the gold medal?' asked Bib sourly. 'It's easy to see that I'm the best competitor round here!'

'No,' replied Bulge firmly while Zainab, Mash and the rest glared angrily at Bib.

Crust stepped forward and grabbed two of Twang's tentacles, one long, one short.

As Twang started thrashing about, it became instantly clear that Crust was perfectly suited to this event. His vice-like grip enabled him to hold on, even when Twang exerted himself to the peak of his bucking capabilities. Crust knocked up the colossal time of fifty-one seconds before Twang managed to dislodge him.

'The winner!' shouted Coach Bulge, walking straight past Bib and draping a gold medal around Crust's neck.

'YESSSSS!' cried Crust, punching the air.

The others ran over to congratulate him, all except for one.

'I'LL SHOW YOU!' shouted Bib, storming out of the barn in a cloud of fury.

6

By the time they got back to the canteen, Chef Cutlass had fixed the wall and was ready to fire Floop stew portions from his Splatter. After a fierce battle, Zainab managed to grab four portions, her best haul so far. After lunch she and Mash relaxed in the sun just outside the Olympic Centre's front door.

'I can't wait till midnight,' said Mash. 'I'll be the first Flamby monster ever to taste a Caramel Marvel.'

'Definitely!' grinned Zainab. 'Talk about a brilliant hiding place!'

'It was amazing seeing you hanging from that hatch above Coach Bulge's head this morning!' said Mash.

They looked at each other and burst out laughing.

'What's so funny?' asked Bib, poking his head round the front door.

'Nothing,' replied Mash quickly.

'Suit yourself!' snapped Bib, pulling a snooty face at them and heading off.

'Do you think he heard us talking about the hatch?' asked Zainab a minute or so after Bib had gone.

'Nah,' said Mash, 'we were whispering.'

Zainab hoped Mash was right, but she couldn't be sure.

*

'Welcome to Event Number Three!' declared Coach Bulge.

Bulge and the nine contestants were standing in a long pit covered with dark red sand. Nine lanes had been marked out by the silver, fork-like bushes Zainab had seen on her first night. The bushes were chatting to each other and laughing in shrill voices. Along each lane was a series of wonky white plinths like the ones you get in museum display cases. On top of these were lots of small, very colourful eggs.

'Can you lot be quiet for a minute while I explain the event to the contestants?' shouted Bulge at the bushes.

The bushes gasped as if they'd just been mortally offended, but they quietened down.

'I have placed one hundred eggs from the Slimba bird on each plinth,' explained Bulge. 'You have fifteen minutes to collect as many eggs as you can with your trunks. Broken eggs and dropped eggs will NOT count. The contestant with most eggs at the finish will be our gold medallist.'

'Er ... what do the Slimba birds have to say about us collecting their eggs?' asked Zainab.

'We produce over five hundred edible eggs per *day*,' declared a huge bird from a branch of a twisted tree, high above the contestants. It was amber in colour and its head was making quick chicken-like movements from side to side. 'You're doing us a favour, believe me!'

'Zainab,' said Bulge, 'as the human nose doesn't have quite the same capabilities as our trunks, I've brought you this. You may carry it in your mouth, both to knock the eggs off and to catch them.'

She handed Zainab a large sieve.

'Thanks, Coach,' nodded Zainab. She placed the sieve in her mouth. Its handle tasted of roast Floop but she was so used to the stuff by now that it didn't bother her.

'Take your places, please!' ordered Bulge.

The contestants fanned out and everyone took a lane.

'Three, two, one, GO!'

Zainab copied all of the monsters, who fell to their knees and started crawling down their lanes. By each plinth they grabbed the eggs and stashed them into various sections of their trunks, which were appearing and disappearing at a frantic rate.

The sieve wasn't quite as good as a multipart

trunk. But it did the job.

Zainab found that by gently knocking the eggs with the sieve she had just enough time to swing it over to catch them as they fell off the plinths. She dropped some and a few broke but her sieve started to fill up.

For ten minutes the lanes kept their shape, but after that the silver fork bushes either got bored or mischievous because they started lying down, jumping on top of each other or simply wandering off. Coach Bulge raced around frantically, trying to round them up, but it was no good. By the time the fifteen minutes were up there were only a handful of bushes in the right place.

'AND STOP!' barked Coach Bulge.

The contestants froze.

'EVERYONE BACK TO THE START LINE!'

When everyone was lined up again, Bulge declared: 'Trunks and sieve at the ready, please!'

She approached the contestants one by one. They shook all of their eggs out of their trunks and into a glass pot with their name on. Zainab was last and she tipped out about two hundred eggs, which she was very pleased with.

Bulge studied the egg levels in every jar and announced that Mash, Arg and Bib had collected the most. Mash clenched his fingers and his toes with nervous excitement. There was a tense silence as Coach Bulge counted their individual collections.

'The winner by one egg,' declared Bulge, 'is ...'

Zainab watched as Mash stuck his head forward in anticipation.

'... is ... Arg!'

'Bonanza!' cried Arg with delight as Bulge placed the third gold medal over her head.

Despair covered Mash's face and his body sagged with disappointment.

'It was fixed!' seethed Bib with a surly expression.

'Don't worry,' said Zainab, giving Mash a pat on the back. 'There are still two events left. I bet you win one of them.'

After the supper battle for Floop lasagne, Zainab and Mash stayed in the canteen with Arg, Crust and Rop, playing a Flamby game called *Boswit* which involved one person being blindfolded and trying to tag the others' knees while they tickled him or her with the brush sections of their trunks. They played sixteen rounds and then showed each other tricks they could do with their laser eyes. Zainab then showed them how she could touch her nose with her tongue. The Flambys loved it and spent ages trying to copy her.

At 11.15 everyone started drifting off to bed, except for Zainab and Mash. Zainab checked her watch. 'Come on,' she said, grabbing Mash by the elbow. 'It's midnight soon and we know what we're doing at midnight, don't we?'

They made sure that everyone else was asleep and then crept up to the hatch. A single shaft of moonlight lit up the corridor. Once again, Zainab climbed on to Mash's back and opened the hatch. She climbed in and went over to the spot where she'd left the Caramel Marvels.

But they weren't on the old bamboo table.
They must have fallen off.
She checked the floor beside the table.
Still no Marvels.
She expanded her search and covered a large

area of the attic floor, but there was no sign of the sweets.

'What are you doing?' hissed up Mash. 'Just get the sweets and then we'll eat them!'

But Zainab couldn't find any trace of the delectable snacks. With a very heavy heart she realized that one thing was absolutely clear.

The Caramel Marvels had gone.

And if this wasn't bad enough, as she walked back to the hatch she tripped over a loose floorboard and fell feet first through the hole.

7

Zainab hit the floor with a loud THUD, badly twisting her left ankle.

'OWWW!' she cried.

Mash quickly knelt down beside her. 'Are you OK?' he asked anxiously.

'I'm fine,' grimaced Zainab, getting to her feet. But she could only manage to hobble back to their bedroom, while Mash found a box to stand on so that he could close the hatch. Then he hurried to join her.

'The Caramel Marvels weren't up there,' Zainab said, sitting down on the edge of her bed.

'You're not serious?' replied Mash, his eyes narrowing in anger as he stared at Bib, who was spinning away, deeply asleep.

'He's done it *again*!' groaned Zainab.

They checked Bib's bag and all round his bed, but there was no sign of the Marvels. Then they carried out a full search of their room, the corridor and the canteen, but still found nothing.

'Next time we won't let him out of our sight,' said Mash, thumping his left fist into his right palm. 'That way we'll catch him!'

'There won't be a next time,' replied Zainab quietly. 'All of my grub's gone now.'

Mash's face fell. No grub. No feast. No luscious midnight snacks. This was a sweets disaster.

But their luck changed in the morning, when after a breakfast of Fried Floop Tarts (Zainab didn't move much in the fight because her ankle still hurt), Coach Bulge handed Mash a large parcel, wrapped in brown nettles.

'This just arrived for you,' she said.

Mash raced and Zainab limped, back to their bedroom. Mash tore off the nettles to uncover a large light-blue brick-shaped object covered in red spots. There was a note with it.

'It's a Gumboo from my mum!' squealed Mash excitedly. 'The most delectable Flamby treat ever! The midnight feast is back on!'

'But where are we going to hide it?' asked Zainab.

Mash blinked five times and when the red points of light shone out of his eyes, he used them to burn a small square hole in the bamboo floor of the bedroom. Lifting up the cut-out square he tucked the Gumboo underneath it.

'But Bib will see the marks,' pointed out Zainab.

'No he won't,' chuckled Mash, 'Rop showed me this last night.' He blinked again and traced over the floor marks. The first time he did this nothing happened, but on his second go the lines started fading. By the end of his fifth eye trace they'd completely vanished.

'THAT'S BRILLIANT!' exclaimed Zainab. 'We'll watch Bib all day to make sure he doesn't sneak back up here.'

'And we'll go to bed at exactly the same time as him,' added Mash.

74

'So we *will* get our midnight feast at last!' grinned Zainab.

When everyone gathered in the canteen for the fourth event, Coach Bulge strode straight over to Zainab. 'I'm sorry,' she said, 'but I've seen you limping and you won't be taking part in this morning's race.'

'It's nothing!' protested Zainab.

Bulge shook her head firmly.

'Can't I at least come and watch?' pleaded Zainab.

'No, it's a long walk there and I want you to rest.'

So as everyone else headed down Tuft Volcano to pastures unknown, Zainab flopped miserably down on her bed and started flicking through an athletics magazine. After half an hour she got bored and decided to look for someone to chat to.

'Hey, Chef Cutlass,' she called as she entered the canteen. Cutlass was sitting with his back to her behind the serving counter, doing something with his Splatter.

He spun round and glared at her. 'No one's allowed in here between meals!' he barked angrily. 'Please leave the canteen immediately!'

Zainab was completely taken aback.

What's up with him?

She went outside and sat on top of Tuft Volcano, waiting to catch a glimpse of the others returning. They showed up over an hour and a half later and by the look on Mash's face he clearly hadn't been victorious.

'Twang was involved again,' said Mash when he reached the top of the volcano and slumped down next to Zainab. 'He ran at full speed along this curving track, and whoever held on to his tail for the longest was the winner. Kimban got her second gold medal.'

'Oh, Mash,' said Zainab, putting her arm round his shoulders. 'There's still one event left.'

'I've given up on representing the Flamby

clan at the Northern Monster Olympics,' said Mash forlornly. 'Anyway, how's your ankle?'

'It still hurts a lot,' she replied, making sure Coach Bulge wasn't in earshot.

Mash's expression suddenly changed from dejected to determined. 'Well, even if *I* won't be winning a gold medal here, we can have a go at fixing your ankle. That way we'll give you the best chance of getting a human Olympic recommendation from Bulge.'

So after a lunch of roasted Floop with Floop salad, Mash strode off down the steps of Tuft Volcano, with Zainab hobbling after him.

'I thought we had to keep our eyes on Bib all day?' said Zainab.

'I'll check the Gumboo hole hasn't been meddled with later,' responded Mash, 'but your ankle's more important right now.'

'Where are we going?' asked Zainab.

'You'll see!' answered Mash, striding ahead.

They walked down a sandy track and

followed two winding paths covered in giant stones, with Zainab wincing in pain at every other step. They stopped when they reached one of the frothing pools she'd seen on the night she arrived. Close up it looked like the jacuzzi she'd sat in at her local swimming pool, but the water here was amazingly clear.

'It's a Jubble Juice Pond,' explained Mash.

Zainab looked into the depths and spotted a series of small, fat oval-shaped oily grey and white creatures with long bushy moustaches

and huge circular mouths. They were blowing bubbles up into the pool.

'They're Jubbles,' explained Mash. 'Their juice has amazing healing powers. It should be good for your ankle.'

'But I haven't got a swimming costume,' pointed out Zainab.

'You won't need one,' replied Mash, 'trust me.'

So, very cautiously, Zainab lowered herself in and found she could sit on the floor of the pond, with her back against the side. Being in the water was incredibly relaxing. The bubbles of Jubble juice surrounded her bad ankle and massaged it. Mash then eased himself into the pond and quickly got comfy. They stayed in for twenty minutes and as Zainab slowly climbed out, one of the Jubbles winked at her and mouthed, 'Good luck with that ankle of yours.'

Zainab's clothes were completely drenched but Mash brought out his trunk brush and in thirty seconds brushed every drop of juice off her until she was completely dry.

Gingerly, Zainab put a little pressure on her ankle and felt zero pain. She walked a few paces, then jogged, without any discomfort at all. A few minutes later she managed a short, pain-free run.

'That's INCREDIBLE!' she marvelled.

'Told you,' grinned Mash, 'but now we need to get back and check the Gumboo is still where we put it.'

By the time they got back to base, her ankle felt brilliant.

Coach Bulge was getting everyone ready to set out for the fifth and final event.

'How's that foot of yours?' Bulge asked Zainab.

Zainab ran to a line of silver fork bushes and vaulted over them, landing without even a twinge of pain.

'You're in!' declared Bulge. 'It's now do or die time!'

'What do you think the last event is going to be?' asked Mash nervously, as Bulge unlocked a gate leading to the high fenced-off area with the river that they'd passed the day before. Mash had raced up to their bedroom before they set off and checked the Gumboo – it was still in place.

'I have no idea,' replied Zainab, noticing that although Mash had declared he had no chance of winning the last gold medal, he still had that sparkle of hope in his eyes.

'This way, please!' commanded Bulge,

climbing on to the bottom rung of a very long and wonky bamboo ladder. The contestants followed her and at the top they emerged on to a large wooden platform overlooking the river below. The river flowed in a big oval shape, before snaking off and heading downstream. In the centre of the oval was a clump of thick, bushy and incredibly tall trees. The river's water was very fast flowing and in it Zainab could see a group of gigantic spiky-backed orange creatures with two heads. Each head had a very long mouth with two rows of gleaming, razor-sharp teeth.

'That is the River Velor,' Coach Bulge informed everyone, 'and those creatures are called Pinchettes. They're a bit like your crocodiles, I believe, Zainab.'

Zainab nodded nervously.

'Luckily Pinchettes are strict vegetarians,' went on Bulge, 'so if, during the course of this race, you happen to fall into the river, they will

NOT eat you. However, they *will* let you know
the River Velor is THEIRS and will PINCH
you with their teeth which, believe me, hurts
A LOT!'

'Er, *how* are we racing?' asked Crust.

'With these!' replied Coach Bulge, grabbing
a huge black sack from the floor of the platform
and emptying out a set of sleek silver boards,

about the same length of an ordinary skateboard but twice as wide.

'COOL!' exclaimed Zainab, gazing at the beautifully designed transporters.

'These Zap Boards travel through the air charged by a special electrical current located in a tiny box on their underside,' explained Bulge.

'What?' said Zainab with huge eyes. 'You mean we … fly?'

'That's exactly what I mean,' nodded Bulge. 'The race involves flying three circuits around the oval of the River Velor. First contestant back to this platform bags the gold medal.'

Bib tapped Zainab and Mash on their shoulders. 'This is MY event!' he snarled. 'So BACK OFF!'

'In your dreams!' hissed Zainab.

'What's going on over there?' demanded Bulge, who had started handing out the Zap Boards.

'It's nothing,' said Mash, glaring at Bib.

When Zainab got her board she placed it down on the platform and stood on it. When everyone was standing on theirs, Coach Bulge flicked a switch on a small black control panel she was holding. Lights crackled along the sides of each Zap Board and they rose into the air.

Yes!

'Touch down on the right front of your board to turn right,' instructed Bulge, 'and on the front left to go left.'

Zainab tapped her foot on the front left of her board; it turned left. She did the same on the right side, and it turned right.

'To travel upwards you apply pressure to the very back tip of the board; to go down you do the same on the front tip.'

Zainab put the sole of her right foot at the back of the board and it tilted upwards. She tried the front and it tipped downwards.

'To go forward you jump up and down on that circle in the centre of the board. To slow down you twist your feet on the circle. To brake you kick that square silver panel on the left. Maximum speed is seventy miles an hour. Now give them a go!'

70 MPH! That's serious speed!

Zainab jumped up and down on the centre circle of her Zap Board and it shot forward. She twisted her feet from side to side on the circle and it lost speed.

I'm on a flying skateboard. My friends would KILL to do this!

Mash cruised above her, shrieking with delight.

The sky was filled with boarders turning, swooping and zigzagging.

Coach Bulge gave them ten minutes of practice and then called everyone back on to the platform. Zainab felt adrenalin pulsing through her body as she landed and lined up for the start. Mash winked at her. She gave him a thumbs-up.

'*Bad luck!*' mouthed Bib at them.

'READY?' yelled Bulge, holding the control panel, her finger hovering over the activation button. 'THEN GO!'

The Zap Boards lifted into the air. Zainab rapidly jumped up and down on the centre of her board. She was off! The nine contestants were now speeding above the oval of the River Velor.

Kimban took an early lead but Mash was on her shoulder. Crust and Rop were in third and fourth place. Zainab was in fifth. Bib was just behind her, with Yag, Arg and Flub bringing up the rear.

Zainab sped smoothly for a long stretch, before veering to the right and edging past Rop into fourth place. She was concentrating so hard that she was startled when she looked to her side and saw she was passing the platform.

I've completed the first circuit!

Crust was now in touching distance, but

he gained more speed and shot further ahead. Zainab was focusing so hard on catching Crust that she didn't see Bib closing in. In a flash he whizzed past, cackling with sneering laughter at her. She jumped furiously on her circle but his jumps were more powerful than hers and in a few seconds he'd put some distance between them.

By the end of the second circuit, Kimban was still in the lead – but she was now just a few metres ahead of Mash. Bib had bypassed Crust and was in third place.

And then Bib started making massive leaps on to his circle and his board crashed forward at top speed. Luckily Mash had spotted what Bib was doing and accelerated too. A few seconds later Mash overtook Kimban and grabbed pole position.

But Bib had other plans.

Veering and swerving wildly, with massive leaps on his circle, he drew equal with Mash.

Mash saw him and tried to dart out of his way, but then Bib did something truly despicable.

He slammed into the side of Mash's board.

The force was explosive. Mash teetered and wobbled for a few seconds before he and his board parted company, and both went crashing down towards the gushing waters of the River Velor, and the razor-sharp teeth of the Pinchettes.

The board would be OK because ... it was a board. But Mash would be on the receiving end of some very powerful and very painful pinches – not to mention the fact that he'd lose the race, and Bib would claim the last gold medal.

In other words:

DISASTER!

Zainab acted instantly. She jumped up and down with great force on her centre circle. She accelerated powerfully and then placed all of her weight at the front tip of the board.

She shot downwards, but saw in distress that Mash was about to hit the river to meet the Pinchettes' welcoming party.

I'm never going to make it!

Zainab hopped back on to the centre of her board and leapt up as high as she could, coming crashing down on to the circle. Mash was only metres above the chomping jaws of the Pinchettes, but with a phenomenal burst of speed Zainab dipped under him and crashed into his back. The force of his body nearly knocked her off the back of her board, but by wrapping her arms round his midriff, she was able to steady herself and stay put. Mash's board crashed into the water, but he was now standing on Zainab's board, shaken but fine.

'LEAN BACK!' bellowed Zainab as they crashed towards the gleaming gnash-giving teeth of the Pinchettes.

They both leant back and just as they were about to collide with the Pinchettes, Zainab's board suddenly tilted up and they zoomed skywards, and out of danger.

Mash spun round. 'ZAINAB!' he shouted. 'YOU ROCK! YOU SAVED ME!'

'FORGET ABOUT THAT!' shouted back Zainab. 'LET'S WIN THIS RACE!'

'HOW' cried Mash, who was watching Bib whizzing towards the platform and the finish line.

'JUMP ON THE SPEED CIRCLE!' yelled Zainab.

Mash pounded up and down on the circle. The Zap Board picked up incredible speed and ten seconds later they were closing in on a very smug Bib.

He was a hundred metres from the platform.

Bib took a quick look round and his joyous expression turned sour.

'YOU'LL NEVER CATCH ME!' he shrieked, leaping up and down on the centre of his board. 'THE LAST GOLD MEDAL IS MINE!'

But there were *two* of Zainab and Mash, and by jumping in unison they were able to get their board to go faster than his. Rapidly they closed the gap.

The platform was now just fifty metres away.

'GO RIGHT!' screeched Zainab.

Mash lunged forward on to the right front tip of the board and they swerved violently rightwards.

But Bib crashed right too and blocked their path.

'GET BACK, LOSERS!' he shrieked.

'WE CAN'T PASS HIM!' shouted Mash.

We need more speed!

At that second Zainab had a brainwave. 'SORRY, MASH!' she yelled. 'BUT THIS IS

THE ONLY WAY!'

Leaping into the air she came crashing down on Mash's left foot. He yelped as his funny bone sprang to life and his left foot started smashing up and down on the centre circle of the Zap Board. As this was happening, Zainab threw all of her weight on to the back tip of the board. There was a loud hissing sound and fiery sparks shot out from the underside of the board.

A split second later, the board shot upwards at quite incredible speed. Its sheer power nearly flung Zainab and Mash off, but they clung to each other and shrieked in delight as they flew *above* Bib.

Bib looked up in horror as their board zoomed over him. Mash stamped on the board's front tip and they headed down, landing on the wooden platform with a great crash.

Bib was so busy gaping at them that his board careered into the side of the platform. He wobbled for a second and then toppled right off his board, tumbling through the air and down towards the clutches of the slavering Pinchettes.

This time, however, Zainab didn't perform a rescue mission.

That task was left to a flabbergasted Coach Bulge, who grabbed a spare board and flew at great speed towards the plummeting and screaming Bib. Unfortunately for Bib, Bulge wasn't quite fast enough to stop him hitting the gushing Velor waters. By the time Bulge reached him, he'd hit the water and picked up several nasty pinches. Bulge grabbed Bib by the scruff of the neck and flew up to the platform with him. He was soaking, sizzling with rage and in last place.

'THE RACE IS NULL AND VOID!' he screamed. 'ZAINAB AND MASH CHEATED! THEY FINISHED ON A BOARD *TOGETHER*. THAT IS NOT ALLOWED! I DEMAND THAT THE RACE IS RUN AGAIN!'

'They're not cheats!' said Crust angrily.

The other contestants murmured their
agreement.

'IDIOTS AND LOW LIFES!' snarled Bib.
'GO ON, COACH BULGE. TELL THEM
WE HAVE TO DO IT AGAIN AND THAT
THOSE TWO ARE DISQUALIFIED!'

All eyes turned to face Bulge. Her brow
furrowed in thought. After a silence that seemed
to last a couple of years she finally spoke. 'Two

people finishing on *one* board is not within the letter of the law,' she said slowly.

I don't believe it! Our victory won't count! Bang goes Mash's gold medal!

There was absolute silence all around apart from a great cry of 'YESSSSS!' from Bib.

'However,' said Bulge, 'I believe that deliberately barging someone off their board, knowing that an army of Pinchettes are waiting below to gnash them, is a far worse crime, and because of that I am awarding first place to the contestant who crossed the line first — irrespective of *whose* board they were on. And that contestant is … MASH!!!'

'I'VE WON GOLD!!!' yelled Mash in delight, hugging Zainab then leaping into the air.

'This is yours,' smiled Bulge, placing a gold medal round Mash's neck.

'That is so unfair!' screeched Bib, throwing himself on the platform floor and banging his fists like a mid-tantrum toddler.

'You kept your focus at the end,' smiled Coach Bulge, placing a hand on Mash's shoulder, 'even if there was someone else on the board to help you!'

'Cheers!' gushed Mash delightedly.

'As a joint winner, Zainab, I will be recommending you most highly to the human Olympic authorities,' declared Bulge. 'You have a big sporting future!'

'THANK YOU!' cried Zainab, performing a delighted dance on the spot.

'Oh, and this is for you,' added Bulge, producing another gold medal and putting it round Zainab's neck.

Unreal! thought Zainab, admiring her medal with awe and then jumping on Mash's back.

As the others congratulated Zainab and Mash on their incredible finish and their gold medals, Bib stayed on the floor, pounding his fists and wailing.

As everyone began to make their way down

the ladder, Zainab pulled Mash aside. 'You DID it!' she beamed. 'You're going to the Northern Monster Olympics!'

'I know!' grinned Mash. 'And you're going to be a human Olympic star!'

'What a team!' laughed Zainab. 'Now there's just one more thing we need to do.'

Mash was so delirious with celebrating that he didn't get what she was talking about.

'Tonight,' said Zainab in a low and very serious voice.

'We catch the Olympic thief!'

10

At supper Bib stood by himself muttering about how he'd been cheated out of a gold medal and how all of the others were scoundrels and liars. It was an unusually cold night and a film of ice covered the top of Tuft Volcano. Zainab wore an extra jumper and after a bout of wrestling with Arg, savoured her hot Floop goulash.

The minute Bib made a move, Zainab and Mash followed him – along the corridor and up the stairs. They peeked round the edge of the bedroom door, and watched as he climbed on to his bed, grumbling. It started spinning and it wasn't long before he was fast asleep.

Mash quickly checked the Gumboo hole.

The Gumboo was still safe.

'OK,' whispered Zainab. 'We sit beside the door and watch Bib. That way we'll see when he makes a grab for the grub.'

'Great plan!' yawned Mash, who was still wearing the smile he'd had on his face since Coach Bulge had announced he'd won the Zap Board race.

They sat in silence and waited.

After half an hour Zainab heard Mash snoring. She whacked him in the ribs and he woke up. 'Gold medal salad,' he mumbled happily.

But fifteen minutes later Zainab's eyelids became heavy and she too drifted off.

A swishing sound woke her up. In the darkness she saw the Gumboo travelling through the air towards the window in the clutches of something resembling a fishing rod.

And Bib's bed was empty.

It is him!

'WAKE UP, MASH!' she yelled. 'IT'S BIB! HE'S THE THIEF!'

Mash opened his eyes and stumbled to his feet.

Zainab rushed over to the window and looked down. A shadowy figure wearing a hoodie was retracting the fishing rod implement *and* the Gumboo.

Thinking ultra fast, Zainab leapt across the room, ripped the wonky shelf off its hinges, ran back to the window and jumped out. She arced through the air and hit the ice, the shelf becoming her skateboard. The thief was racing away, the Gumboo in one hand, the fishing rod contraption in the other.

Oh no you don't, Bib!

Zainab zigzagged along the icy ground, determined to capture the midnight-feast-snatcher.

As the thief swerved round a corner, Zainab drew level, leapt off her board and landed on the thief's back, bringing him crashing down on to the icy ground.

Zainab yanked off the thief's hoodie, looking forward to gloating in Bib's smug face.

But she had to stop herself.

Because the thief wasn't Bib.

'CHEF CUTLASS?' cried Zainab.

Mash, who had leapt out of the window to

follow the chase, skidded up beside them. He stood, open-mouthed, staring at the Olympic chef.

'Oh no!' groaned Zainab. 'Chef Cutlass has been stealing our sweets and throwing them away because they're not healthy. Mash – we're in BIG TROUBLE!'

'Er ... it's not quite like that,' replied Cutlass quietly. 'I ... I ... have something to confess.'

Zainab and Mash looked at him in confusion.

'I never was a pirate,' said Cutlass with shame. 'I worked in a pirate-themed café which hosted parties for screaming little monsters. The only thing we served in there were treats – Gumboos, Chapsters, Fin-Fin lollies. You name it – I've eaten it. I ate so much of the stuff that I completely fell in love with everything sweet. As Coach Bulge banned all sweet foods here, I *had* to get my hands on something.'

'But how did you know where to find ours?' asked Mash in amazement. 'I mean, today's hiding place was invisible!'

'You know those little purple boxes on all of the doors?' said Cutlass.

Zainab and Mash nodded.

'They're security cameras,' explained the Chef. 'There's a room just off the kitchen which houses all of the TV monitors linked to the cameras. I was in there on the first night and just happened to see Mash putting your bar of chocolate behind that wall panel in your room. I'd never tasted chocolate so I nipped in and grabbed it when you weren't there. It was truly delicious! After that I kept a very close eye on your movements and saw your ceiling hiding place, and your invisible floor square.'

'And that's why you kicked me out of the canteen yesterday,' murmured Zainab, looking down at the fishing rod contraption, which she now recognized. 'You were adapting your Splatter Gun.'

'Take me to Coach Bulge and I will face my

punishment,' said Cutlass sadly.

'Forget that,' said Zainab, 'have you eaten all of our stuff yet?'

'No,' replied Cutlass sorrowfully, 'I've only made a tiny start.'

'Great!' smiled Zainab. 'Get the rest of it and meet us up in our room in five minutes. That way we can have a midnight feast *together*!'

'You're inviting a thief to share stolen property with its rightful owners?' asked Cutlass slowly.

'Yes,' grinned Zainab.

'Will you tell everyone I was never a pirate?'

'No, me hearty!' smiled Zainab. 'Now go and get the grub.'

'THANK YOU SO MUCH!' cried Cutlass, giving them both body-crunching hugs before racing off to the canteen.

Zainab and Mash headed back into the building. When they entered their room there was still no sign of Bib.

'But if he's not the thief,' pondered Mash, 'where is he?'

They were talking this over when Chef Cutlass burst in, laden with all of their sweetmeats.

'Er, Chef,' said Zainab. 'Do you know where Bib is?'

Cutlass nodded. 'He's down in the kitchen washing all of the dirtiest pots and pans.'

'WHAT?' exclaimed Zainab.

'Coach Bulge got him out of bed and said it's his punishment for cheating.'

Zainab and Mash looked at each other and then burst out laughing.

'Here try this!' said Mash, handing Zainab a slice of the light blue brick – the Gumboo.

She bit off a chunk and rolled it on to her tongue. 'Not bad,' she remarked, as an almond-like flavour danced on her taste buds.

'These are great!' grinned Mash, sampling several Caramel Marvels at the same time.

It took quite some time for the three of them to finish the mountain of goodies, but when they did their bellies were stuffed to the max.

'Thanks for not turning me in,' said Chef Cutlass, getting up to leave.

'No problem!' replied Zainab.

Cutlass grinned and went on his way.

Zainab and Mash stayed up for ages talking about all of the trial events, their gold medals and the Olympic thief. When they finally hit their beds, they drifted off to a deep and contented sleep. This time, though, it wasn't with a bitter taste in their mouths, but with a delicious sugary tang on their lips.

MASH
and the
SINISTER SUPPLY TEACHER

Dear Zainab and family

I'm delighted you've agreed to host the visit of Mash, a monster from the Flamby monster clan, and the monster-exchange partner of Zainab.

Flamby monsters are well known for rushing around and doing things very quickly, so if Mash views some of your behaviour as painfully slow, please do not be offended.

I should warn you that Flambys have very strange habits in relation to eating. Their mealtimes involve a sort of food-firing gun and lots of fighting. If you'd like Mash to eat in a different room (or even a different building) to avoid any battles, that is fine. In addition, the Flambys can only sleep on special spinning beds. I will send you a diagram of one in the hope that you'll be able to provide something suitable for Mash's sleeping arrangements.

Wishing you the very best of luck for Mash's visit.

Yours sincerely

Sir Horace Upton

Human Agency for Understanding Monsters

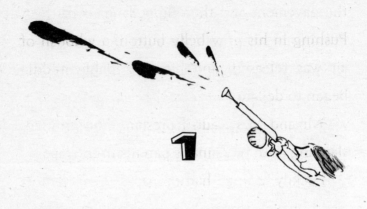

'THERE HE IS!' shouted Zainab excitedly, pointing at the far end of the street.

In the distance, a long purple figure was bouncing along the top of a bus, on its hugely inflated circular belly. As it reached the end of the bus's roof it launched itself through the air and belly-flopped on to the bus in front.

'That doesn't look awfully safe,' said Zainab's mother nervously.

'It's *totally* safe!' replied Zainab as the creature bounced on to a further three buses before drawing parallel with the Kaur family. He threw himself off the bus, bounced three times on the pavement and then flipped on to his feet. Pushing in his grey belly button, a whoosh of air was released, and his expandable middle began to deflate.

'Mr and Mrs Kaur, I presume?' he grinned, slapping both of Zainab's parents in the face.

Luckily, Zainab had prepared them for this traditional Flamby greeting and they responded by slapping him back. Mash and Zainab then exchanged hearty face slaps.

'Welcome, Mash!' smiled Mr Kaur.

'Zainab has told us so much about you!' added Mrs Kaur.

'It's supreme to be here!' grinned Mash. 'Are we heading straight to your school, Zainab?'

'Yeah!' replied Zainab, taking him by the elbow and heading off down the street with her parents following behind.

'You'll love my teacher, Mr Armoury,' said Zainab. 'He's really cool! He flies an old Spitfire plane at the weekends and takes us on amazing trips!'

'Excellent!' laughed Mash, breaking into a run, his long wavy legs and sausage-shaped toes pounding the pavement.

Ten minutes later, they arrived outside the gates of Willow Street Primary School – a one storey, reddish-brown building.

'Be good, Zainab,' said her father.

'Look after Mash at all times,' added her mother. 'He's a very special guest.'

'Yes, Mum! Yes, Dad!' groaned Zainab. 'We'll see you later.'

'Bye, Mash!' called Mr and Mrs Kaur, waving their daughter's monster friend off.

Mash gave Zainab's parents his brightest smile, then he and Zainab ran down the path and disappeared inside the building after a gaggle of children up ahead.

By the time they reached the playground it was pretty full, with children clustered in groups – talking, shouting at each other, playing football, skipping, running, and climbing on the castle play-frame. There were lots of mums and dads milling around, talking about which teacher they were most scared of.

The second Mash appeared, excited whispers spread like a bush fire across the tarmac and in less than thirty seconds everyone had stopped what they were doing and were gaping at the new arrival.

'Hi, everyone!' grinned Mash, giving them a

wave with one of his tiny three-fingered hands. 'I'm Mash, from the Flamby monster clan!'

A split second later every child and adult, in an attempt to greet the monster, rushed towards Mash at top speed (they'd all been told about his visit and were stupendously excited).

In no time at all Mash and Zainab were completely surrounded and Mash was being bombarded with questions and requests.

'I LOVE your ear hair, Mash! Is it natural?' yelled Annabel Prentice.

'Have you tried tomato and garlic crisps? I have some in my bag!' shouted Robbie Percival.

'Mash, can I photograph your legs?' bellowed Arjun Singh.

As more and more people arrived at school, the crowd around Mash and Zainab got bigger and bigger and more hysterical.

'GIVE HIM SOME SPACE!' cried Zainab, as the throng penned them in. But no one heard her over the deafening crescendo of noise.

At first Mash loved all the attention and beamed with pride, but after a while it became too much even for him. 'We need to get away from here!' bellowed Zainab.

'We'll have to use brute force!' Mash shouted as he was flung from side to side and from back to front.

He and Zainab lowered their heads like a pair of battle-ready bulls, and charged. The crowd were barged out of the way as the human-monster team smashed out a path for themselves and began running off down the playground.

'WAIT!' screamed the masses, chasing after them.

'This is RIDICULOUS!' yelled Zainab, looking over her shoulder and seeing the advancing hordes. 'We've got to put something between us and them or they'll crush us to a pulp!'

As they approached the castle play-frame, Mash grabbed it and completely uprooted it. He swung it behind him like a knight's mace, which forced lots of their pursuers to leap backwards to avoid being clonked.

This gave Zainab and Mash a bit of breathing space, but there was one small problem: there were several children *on* the play-frame.

A few were terrified and screamed, 'LET US OFF OR WE'LL DIE!'

But the rest were ecstatic and screamed, 'AN AWESOME FLYING CASTLE! PLEASE DON'T STOP!'

On ran Zainab and Mash, twisting this way and that, the play-frame swinging in their wake. But some of the chasers started running to the side and then forward, avoiding the play-frame and gaining on Zainab and Mash.

'We've got to DO something else!' shouted Zainab urgently.

But before she and Mash could decide on a new strategy, a clear and thunderous voice rose above the melee and yelled:

'STOP THIS AT ONCE!'

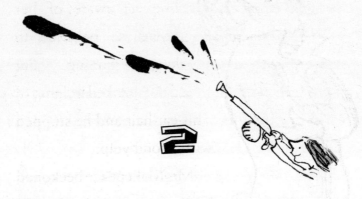

2

Every child and adult who was sprinting after Mash and Zainab suddenly braked to a crunching halt.

That was because the clear and thunderous voice belonged to Mrs Makepeace, the head teacher of Willow Street Primary. She was small in size but vast in power – a raised eyebrow from her could reduce even the toughest kids to sobbing wrecks. She was wearing a light blue skirt suit, her blonde hair tucked into a neat bunch, and a deep, disapproving frown on her face.

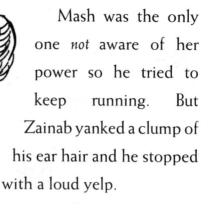

Mash was the only one *not* aware of her power so he tried to keep running. But Zainab yanked a clump of his ear hair and he stopped with a loud yelp.

Mrs Makepeace beckoned Mash and Zainab towards her with a thin, curled finger. All eyes in the playground were glued to their every step. When they reached her she leaned forward and spoke in a very low tone so that only they could hear her.

'I'm Mrs Makepeace, and it's lovely to meet you, Mash.'

Zainab saw Mash's hand rising to slap the head teacher's cheek, but she grabbed it in the nick of time.

'I must apologize for the behaviour of my pupils and their parents,' said Mrs Makepeace.

'No problem at all, Mrs M,' grinned Mash.

'However,' continued the head teacher, 'I cannot have you uprooting playground equipment and swinging it around your head, as this breaches certain health and safety regulations.'

'Understood!' replied Mash, dropping the castle play-frame on to the ground with a loud thud. The terrified children jumped off and ran to their parents, shrieking. The others groaned in disappointment because their ride was over.

'So long as you stick to certain school rules, I'm sure you will have an excellent stay,' smiled Mrs Makepeace, 'so I extend our warmest welcome.'

Mash wriggled his trunk in thanks.

Mrs Makepeace then turned to face everyone else in the playground. 'I know you're all very excited about Mash's arrival,' she declared, 'but that does NOT give you the right to chase after him screaming at the top of your voices in an attempt to smother him. Imagine if it was *you* going to a Flamby monster school and you were chased by crazed hordes on your first morning!'

Lots of children gulped and several parents looked down at the ground in shame.

'Now,' went on Mrs Makepeace, 'parents, could I ask you to leave, and children, please line up with your classes.'

As Zainab and Mash walked over to join Mr Armoury's line, lots of kids in the class smiled at Mash, waved greetings and gave him friendly pats on the back, but no one tried to crush him. He smiled, slapped a few of their faces and tickled Eddie Wright under the chin with the brush section of his trunk.

'Mr Armoury will be here in a second,' grinned Zainab.

But Mr Armoury did *not* show up. Instead it was Mrs Makepeace who appeared at the front of their line.

'Where's Mr Armoury?' called Zainab.

'All will become clear in a few moments,' replied Mrs Makepeace, 'but first I want you inside and at your tables.'

Two minutes later everyone was in the classroom. Danny Nolan had moved from his place so that Mash could sit next to Zainab.

'I got a call early this morning telling me that a place had just become available on a course run by the legendary teacher-trainer, Hattie Practice,' began Mrs Makepeace. 'She asked if I would like any teacher from this school to take up the place, and I said yes, I would like Mr Armoury to go. As a result, Mr Armoury will be away on Hattie Practice's course this week.'

There were groans all round the class, none louder than Zainab's.

'The whole week!' cried Zainab. 'That's so not fair! Mash won't get a chance to meet him!'

'It's not the end of the world,' said Mrs Makepeace firmly, 'and anyway, the supply

128

teacher I've booked comes with a first-class reputation. Apparently he was at teacher-training college with Mr Armoury.'

There were murmurs all round.

'Well,' sighed Zainab, 'if he's a friend of Mr Armoury, he should be OK.'

'He's having a look through your books at this very minute,' went on the head teacher, 'so he'll have a good idea of the wonderful work you all do. In fact, he's here right now!'

A tall, wiry man, with dark green eyes, thin lips and a 'c'-shaped dimple on his chin entered the classroom. He was wearing an immaculate light grey and black pinstriped suit and was carrying a mound of exercise books.

'Mr Sharpish!' beamed Mrs Makepeace, 'I've just been telling the children about you training to be a teacher with Mr Armoury.'

'That's right,' smiled Mr Sharpish. 'I'm very familiar with Mr Armoury's teaching methods. And I now know the kind of things he's been doing with all of *you*.'

He beamed at the class.

'Excellent!' nodded Mrs Makepeace approvingly. 'As you can see, Mr Sharpish, we have an additional member of class this week. Mash is the monster I told you about on the phone. He is the exchange partner of Zainab.'

Mr Sharpish turned to face Mash and Zainab and gave them a tooth-whitening smile.

Mash wiggled his ear hair by way of a greeting, which got a big laugh from the class.

'Right,' nodded Mrs Makepeace. 'I'll leave you to it, Mr Sharpish. I'm sure you'll all have a wonderful time together!'

'We will indeed!' smiled Mr Sharpish, waving at her enthusiastically as she left the class. The smile stayed on his face until she was out of sight.

It was then replaced with a sneering glare.

'Oh, I know Mr Armoury's teaching methods all right!' snapped Mr Sharpish. *Let's paint our ears and pretend we're insects! Let's wear cereal packets and imagine we're pilots flying into enemy territory!'*

'Mr Armoury's a brilliant teacher!' cried Zainab in shock.

'Brilliant at being terrible!' snapped Mr Sharpish. 'I've looked through your books and I can't believe it. Where are the pages of sums? Where are the hundreds of lines of handwriting practice? What does Mr Armoury think this place is – a zoo?'

The children and Mash stared at him in fury.

I know humans are different but he's downright <u>nasty</u>, thought Mash.

'When I heard he was away for a whole week, I leapt at the opportunity to hammer some _proper_ education into the minds of his neglected pupils – i.e. YOU!'

'You can't say those things about Mr Armoury!' exclaimed Danny Nolan.

'I can say whatever I like!' snarled Mr Sharpish, licking his lips like a ravenous fox entering an unguarded chicken coop. 'You have been taught the *wrong* way!'

'But ... but ...' said Zainab.

'But nothing!' bellowed Mr Sharpish. 'For the duration of my stay here, every single one of you will do things the *right* way. And just to avoid any misunderstandings – the right way is

MY WAY!'

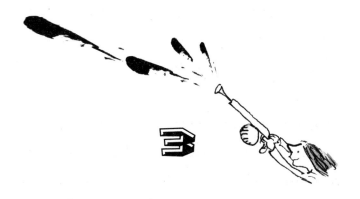

The whole class sat in dumbfounded silence.

'I am the greatest teacher you will EVER meet,' went on Mr Sharpish, preening himself like a boastful peacock. 'MY REPUTATION IS SECOND TO NONE! No child – human or monster – has EVER got the better of me!'

Mash and Zainab looked at each other in horror.

Mr Sharpish then turned his glare on Mash. 'I would imagine monsters are taught *nothing* apart from belching and eating dirty shrubs!'

'That's only in our first year of school!' protested Mash.

Mr Sharpish ignored him, reached into his briefcase and pulled out a pile of thick maths booklets that he proceeded to throw at each child.

Zainab caught hers and had a quick flick through it.

'Er ... we haven't covered lots of this stuff yet,' she piped up.

'If Mr Armoury has failed to teach you certain basic mathematical principles, then that's *his* lookout and *your* problem!' snapped Mr Sharpish. 'Now get on with your work and don't make a sound!'

After a lot of huffing everyone opened their booklets and began to wade through the hundreds of sums.

Mash gripped a pencil with the knitting-needles section of his trunk and started whizzing through the booklet, his trunk glowing slightly.

'Maths is my best subject,' he whispered to Zainab. 'In my school I won the prize for the biggest collection of porcupig bogies.'

'What's a porcupig?' asked Zainab.

'A cross between a porcupine and a pig,' replied Mash, 'spiky *and* smelly.'

Zainab giggled.

'WHAT DO YOU THINK YOU'RE DOING?' demanded Mr Sharpish, marching

over and snatching the pencil from Mash's trunk.

'This is how we write in my monster clan,' explained Mash.

'In case you hadn't noticed, you are NOT in your monster clan now,' hissed the venomous supply teacher. 'You are in the *human* world, so you will write like us!'

'But that's unfair!' piped up Zainab.

'I will not tolerate IMPUDENCE!' shouted Mr Sharpish, yanking the pencil out of Mash's trunk. Mash gritted his teeth and began the fiendishly difficult task of trying to write with his tiny fingers. From working at super speed he was reduced to going ultra slow.

At half past ten Zainab and the rest of the class started getting ready for break, but Mr Sharpish rapped a metal metre ruler on his desk.

'No break for lazy ignoramuses!' he declared, his dark green eyes blazing with contempt.

'This is a complete nightmare!' hissed Zainab.

'It's the pits!' whispered Mash back, thinking, *How I'd love to whack him with the mallet part of my trunk!*

When lunchtime finally came round, Mr Sharpish snatched up the ashen-faced children's booklets and yelled, 'DISAPPEAR FROM MY SIGHT IMMEDIATELY!'

*

'We *have* to get rid of him!' said Zainab, as the class huddled together miserably in the playground.

'But how?' asked Eddie Wright.

'I could hang him up on the school flag pole by the scruff of the neck,' offered Mash.

'Tempting,' said Zainab, 'but Mrs Makepeace would go crazy. We need something more subtle.'

They all threw in lots of ideas but none of them was quite good enough. When it was time to eat, Mash stood in the canteen, flexing his muscles and getting ready for the canteen staff to fire the food with a Splatter Gun.

'We don't fight for our food here,' explained Zainab, tugging him into the queue. 'We get served and then we sit down and eat it off plates.'

After eating a large plate of pizza and vegetables, followed by a portion of apple pie, Mash swept some crumbs off Eddie Wright's face with the brush section of his trunk and ate them.

Shame about the lack of fighting, thought Mash, *but the food was OK, considering it wasn't made of Floop.*

By the end of lunchtime the class still hadn't come up with anything clever enough to thwart their destructive supply teacher, so they trooped back into class with heavy hearts and long faces.

'Right,' announced Mr Sharpish, holding up one of the maths booklets. 'This is Carly Adams' work.'

He fanned himself with it before tearing it to shreds, and throwing the pieces in the air.

They floated to the ground like multiplication confetti.

'Hey!' protested Carly. 'I got some of those sums right!'

'*Some* is as good as NOTHING!' snarled Mr Sharpish, his thin lips curved into a hateful glare. 'Carly Adams – YOU FAIL!'

Next he held up Robbie Percival's booklet and tore it to pieces. 'Robbie Percival – YOU FAIL!'

Robbie opened his mouth to protest, but he was so stunned that no words emerged.

Then came Zainab's booklet. 'Zainab Kaur – YOU FAIL!'

Three minutes later every child's booklet lay in tatters on the classroom floor.

'The trouble with you lot,' sneered Mr Sharpish, 'is that Mr Armoury has given you no backbone.'

'My backbones are quite all right,' said Mash, standing up, turning round and demonstrating the almost-perfectly straight set of knobbly bones snaking down his back.

Zainab and a few of the others giggled, but Mr Sharpish whacked his metre ruler on the desk again. 'It's time that you undertook some character-building tasks,' he declared. 'Your playground is filthy. You are to pick up every piece of litter with these!'

From his jacket pocket he pulled out a box of toothpicks and handed two to every child.

'You're joking, right?' said an incredulous Zainab.

'Do I look like I'm joking?' hissed the crazed teacher.

Mr Sharpish led the class outside and looked at his watch. 'You have ten minutes!' he snapped. 'If I find one piece of litter in this playground at inspection time, you will all receive a three-hour detention after school!'

He chuckled to himself and went back inside.

'We'll never do it!' groaned Zainab, as the class surveyed the mass of playground litter. It was in the bushes, on the tarmac and clogging up the drains.

'Yes we will!' replied Mash with a sly grin.

'How?' asked Zainab.

'As long as someone keeps an eye on Mr Sharpish, I'll do the job much quicker than all of you put together.'

I'll get the better of this horrible human-education man!

So while Zainab ran off to spy on Mr Sharpish and make sure he stayed in the classroom, Mash pressed his belly button and inflated his midriff with a whoosh of air. A second later, he was bouncing around the playground on his stomach at incredible speed, picking up litter with various sections of his multipart trunk and depositing them in the red playground dustbins.

Ten minutes later, when Mr Sharpish came out for the inspection, the class were standing in a neat line, toothpicks held smartly in the air, eyes glazed over like robotic servants. He surveyed the spotlessly clean playground. His face went red then purple then red again and he muttered furiously under his breath.

'Right, this way!' he thundered, leading them into the hall. He pointed to the high, dirty windowpanes. 'Let's see if you can clean every window in the hall using only these!'

He pulled a yellow cloth out of his jacket pocket, cut it into thirty-one tiny pieces and handed a piece to each child and one to Mash. 'For this task you have just seven minutes!' he barked at them before marching out.

As soon as he was out of sight Mash took charge once again, bouncing high round the hall on his belly, using all the cloths at the same time with different parts of his trunk.

When Mr Sharpish returned he was nearly blinded by the gleaming windows.

His face contorted with rage, and his fists clenched with fury. 'So you managed to complete a couple of ridiculously easy tasks!' he bellowed. 'BIG DEAL! If you think you've got the better of me you are very WRONG. As soon as I get evidence proving what a badly-taught and ill-disciplined rabble you are, I will present this information to Mrs Makepeace, who will be forced to sack Mr Armoury and hire me as his replacement!'

There was a collective in-breath of shock from the children.

Mr Sharpish checked the clock and saw it was the end of the day. 'NOW BE GONE!' he cried.

Most of the class were so relieved to be going home that they raced away from the building as fast as they could.

But Zainab had other plans.

'We've only had *one* day with Mr Sharpish!' she groaned to Mash. 'Another four days will kill us!'

'But what can we do?' asked Mash. 'No one's come up with a genius plan yet.'

'We're going to the top,' said Zainab with grim determination. She strode off down the corridor with Mash hot on her heels.

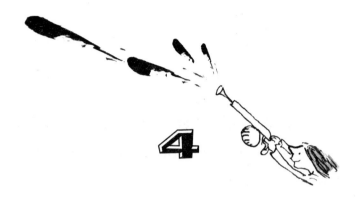

Zainab rapped her knuckles on Mrs Makepeace's door.

'COME IN!' called the head teacher.

Zainab and Mash stepped inside, shutting the door behind them.

Mrs Makepeace looked up from her computer screen. 'Ah, Mash, how was your first day?'

'It sucked!' replied Mash.

'Really?' frowned Mrs Makepeace. 'Why was that?'

'Mr Sharpish is horrible, mean and cruel!' seethed Mash.

Mrs Makepeace looked shocked.

'He's right,' nodded Zainab. 'Mr Sharpish is awful. He ripped up our maths booklets even though we got lots of sums right, and he made us clean the playground with toothpicks!'

Mrs Makepeace eyed Zainab warily. 'Look, Zainab,' she replied, 'I know how much your class like Mr Armoury, but making up stories about Mr Sharpish won't help matters.'

'They're not stories!' protested Mash.

'Can't you just get rid of Mr Sharpish and bring back Mr Armoury?' pleaded Zainab. 'You could tell Mr Armoury that you need him here more than on that course?'

'I'm sorry,' replied the head teacher in her firmest voice, 'but Mr Armoury will complete his course and Mr Sharpish will be with you for the rest of the week. And that is final!'

*

'It's SO unfair!' complained Zainab as she and Mash walked home. 'The one time you come to

146

visit we get Mr Sharpish!'

'We *have* to defeat him,' said Mash grimly.

'My reputation is second to none!' mimicked Zainab.

She and Mash burst out into peals of laughter. It was the first time they'd laughed since the beginning of the school day.

'WE'RE HOME!' called Zainab as they entered the Kaur household.

'How did it go?' asked Mrs Kaur, coming out of the kitchen and wiping her hands on an apron.

'It was …OK,' replied Mash.

He and Zainab had agreed not to tell the truth to Zainab's mum and dad. If they did and her parents complained to Mrs Makepeace, it might make matters even worse.

'Just OK?' asked Zainab's mum.

'Mr Armoury's away on a course so we have a supply teacher,' said Zainab quickly, grabbing Mash's elbow and charging upstairs.

'Supper will be ready in half an hour,' shouted Mrs Kaur after them.

At the top of the stairs they ran into Zainab's bedroom. Mash stopped beside a two-tiered wooden contraption. 'What's that?' he asked, eyeing it with interest.

'It's a bunk bed,' replied Zainab, climbing on to the upper bunk. 'I sleep on the top one and if friends come to stay, they get the bottom one.'

'I don't think I'll fit in there,' said Mash doubtfully.

'You won't have to,' replied Zainab. 'Your bed is over *there*.'

Mash turned round and on the floor by the window he saw a large oval of wood mounted on a circular metal base. Zainab's dad had made it and rigged it up so that the base rotated. It was a perfect Flamby bed!

'Excellent!' beamed Mash, leaping on to it and having a quick spin.

Next he ran over to Zainab's cupboard,

yanked open the door and gazed inside. The shelves were filled with neatly folded jumpers, hoodies, trousers and an assortment of other clothes.

How many sets of clothes can one human need? One set of fur's enough for me!

He placed a pair of Zainab's jeans on his head, a blue velvet hat on his trunk, an orange sock on each hand, and then started jumping round the room singing, 'I'M A HUMAN! OH

YEAH! I'M A H-U-M-A-N!'

Zainab laughed so loudly she fell off the top bunk. She then chucked Mash one of her earphone buds, while she kept the other, and they listened to some songs on her MP3 player while dancing round the room.

A short while later, Mrs Kaur called them down for supper. Having sat down for lunch at school, Mash was already getting used to not battling for his food, and he ate several of Mrs Kaur's pancakes with relish.

'I hear Mr Armoury's away for the week,' said Zainab's dad, who'd just got in from work.

Zainab exchanged a glance with Mash, but said nothing.

When they'd finished eating Zainab cleared the table while Mash used the screwdriver section of his trunk and a tea towel to dry the dishes in record time. They then went to the sitting room and flopped down in front of the telly to watch a programme about Olympic running legends.

As it was finishing, Zainab's dad poked his head round the door.

'I just got a phone call from your supply teacher, Mr Sharpish,' he said.

Zainab and Mash sat up instantly, their smiles vanishing.

'He asked if I could sign a piece of paper granting permission for both of you to go on a class trip tomorrow.'

'What did you say?' asked Zainab.

'I said yes,' replied Mr Kaur. 'Is that OK?'

Zainab and Mash both nodded slowly, unsure how to take this news.

'Anyway, it's time for you two to go to bed,' said Zainab's dad.

'Not yet!' pleaded Zainab, '*Smash your Swimming Instructor* is on next!'

'Yes yet!' replied Mr Kaur firmly, switching off the TV.

Zainab howled the universally recognized

anguished sound that greets any adult when they extinguish any type of screen.

'Good night, you two!' called Mrs Kaur from the study, where she was catching up on some work on her laptop.

They raced up to the bathroom. As Zainab brushed her teeth at the sink Mash knelt down and stuck his head into the toilet bowl.

'What are you doing?' blurted out Zainab, spitting toothpaste everywhere.

'I'm giving my head hair a wash before bed,' replied Mash, flicking his head back and splashing toilet water everywhere.

'Er ... wrong water,' said Zainab, who insisted on washing Mash's single hair and the rest of his head with shampoo and then rinsing it under the tap, before chucking him a towel.

A few minutes later, Zainab was tucked up in her top bunk and Mash was spinning round on his rotating bed. It wasn't quite as fast as his bed back home, but it would definitely do.

'Where do you think Mr Sharpish is going to take us on the trip?' asked Mash, after Zainab had turned out the light.

'I have no idea,' yawned Zainab, 'but it's bound to be deeply unpleasant.'

A few seconds later Zainab was fast asleep.

Mash lay awake for a good while, spinning round and wondering what frightful tasks the evil supply teacher would have in store for them the following day.

'Hurry up!' ordered Mr Sharpish, leading Mr Armoury's class out through the school gates and down the road to the train station, straight after taking the register.

'Where are we going?' asked Zainab.

'The Museum of Natural History,' snapped Mr Sharpish, 'for a dose of *proper* learning!'

On the train, Mr Sharpish walked among the pupils, hissing at them to quieten down, because: 'MY REPUTATION IS SECOND TO NONE!'

Thirty minutes later, they were standing in

the very high and very echoey forecourt of the museum.

'Right,' announced Mr Sharpish, handing out clipboards with very thick workbooks attached. 'So that I can show Mrs Makepeace what you are *really* like, I have provided you with a series of activities to complete. The first involves answering all of the questions about rivers and oceans on pages one to nine of your workbooks. You have thirty minutes! Now scram!'

'Come on!' called Zainab as she, Mash and the rest of the class raced to the rivers and oceans section. As soon as they opened their booklets they saw the hugeness of the task Mr Sharpish had set them.

'We'll never answer all of these questions in half an hour,' groaned Robbie Percival.

'We will if we split up the questions and help each other,' Zainab replied.

It only took her and Mash a few moments to share out the questions. The class fanned

out round the area and began writing furiously. But when a gleeful Mr Sharpish appeared thirty minutes later, they were nowhere near finished.

'Just as I thought,' he grinned. 'You FAIL!'

'We just need a bit more time!' protested Zainab.

'SILENCE!' barked Mr Sharpish. 'The questions on pages ten to twenty of your booklets relate to the museum's dinosaur collection. You have twenty minutes to complete those, starting NOW!'

But once again, even though they pooled their answers together, the task was nowhere near finished by the time Mr Sharpish appeared.

'YOU FAIL!' he yelled again with delight.

Following this, the class had to:

* Write a five-page review of a film on the life cycle of the lower spotted Mandrogal plant. '**YOU FAIL!**' bellowed Mr Sharpish.

* Create a film script based on eight characters in the Roman fish-farming display. '**YOU FAIL!**' gloated Mr Sharpish.

* Complete a complex comprehension task about the bones of loose-jawed, elderly crocodiles. '**YOU FAIL!**' snapped Mr Sharpish.

They were then allowed just fifteen minutes for lunch, after which Mr Sharpish sent them off to compose seven letters that could have been written by seven different Inca tribesmen to members of their families.

'Here he is again!' seethed Zainab when Mr Sharpish showed up to declare 'YOU FAIL!' for the sixth time.

I've had enough of this, thought Mash furiously. *It's time for us to get our own back on him!*

'Your final task is about earthquakes,' announced Mr Sharpish. 'You will write twenty paragraphs of earthquake information in six minutes!'

The class hurried over to the earthquake section and began scribbling down earthquake facts. Mash and Zainab, however, wrote nothing. Instead, they stood staring at the Earthquake Simulator – a large, black, raised rectangular platform.

'Go on it for a minute,' Zainab said to Mash,

a flicker of an idea igniting in her brain.

As soon as Mash was standing on the platform, Zainab pressed the SIMULATOR START button. The platform began to judder and twist – supposedly creating the feeling of what it was like to be caught in the middle of a mild earthquake. But its jolts and turns were pretty tame and Mash had no trouble remaining upright.

As he jumped off the platform he noticed a fiendish grin spreading across Zainab's face. Her eyes were following a series of cables that stretched from the bottom of the simulator to a junction box fixed on to a large pillar. An armful of pennies suddenly dropped in Mash's mind.

She's thinking of turning this slow human simulator into a fizzing breakneck machine!

'You're not serious?' he asked.

'I'm deadly serious,' replied Zainab. 'Do you think you can change the Simulator's settings?'

'I'll give it a go,' nodded Mash eagerly.

'Great,' replied Zainab. 'You tinker with the junction box, I'll find Eddie and Robbie and get them on to the Simulator at normal speed. Then I'll fetch Mr Sharpish for a daredevil ride!'

'Got it!' replied Mash, his ear hair rippling with excitement.

So as Zainab raced off to complete her part of the plan, Mash hurried over to the junction box. Making sure that no one was watching, he extended the screwdriver section of his trunk, undid some screws and flicked open the metal cover.

A couple of minutes later Zainab reappeared with Mr Sharpish striding at her side. The Earthquake Simulator was on, and with superb pieces of acting, Eddie and Robbie were lurching, swerving and continually falling over, whimpering, 'Someone help us!' even though the platform was going at its normal, mild pace.

'THAT'S NOT THE WAY YOU DO IT!' shouted Mr Sharpish. 'Get off at once and let the master demonstrate!'

Eddie and Robbie half stumbled, half fell off the Simulator. Mr Sharpish shoved them aside and leapt on to it.

'The secret is perfect balance,' he boasted, bending his knees and holding his arms out to steady himself. The twists and the turns of the platform didn't affect his balance at all and he smiled smugly as the whole class gathered round the Simulator to watch him.

Hidden behind the pillar, Mash used his trunk pliers to turn a large black dial. The earthquake floor panel upped its speed, twisting, dipping and rotating. Mr Sharpish looked surprised, but he managed to keep his balance.

Mash turned the dial again.

The earthquake platform sped up again, but Mr Sharpish still managed to stay put.

Then suddenly, after Mash gave the dial a big turn, the platform went completely crazy, smashing this way and that, rising and falling at phenomenal speed. Mr Sharpish rearranged his feet and changed his posture, crouching lower to keep his balance. Sweat was pouring off his forehead, and his eyes looked manic.

Mash's trunk pliers then performed a final dial twist.

The platform smashed out of control. Mr Sharpish was now just a blurred figure, desperately reaching out for something to grab hold of.

But there was only air.

With a colossal jolt of power, the platform floor jerked backwards and then shot forwards, propelling the hapless supply teacher through the air like a catapult. He flew out of the earthquake section, over the huge skeleton of a T Rex, and into the café area, where he landed head first in a gigantic green food-recycling bin.

6

Mash and Zainab raised their fists in triumph and the rest of the class cheered with delight. But as Mash ran over to turn the dial back to its normal setting and re-seal the junction box, a horrible primeval roar rose up from the direction of the museum's café.

Loud soggy footsteps echoed round the museum as the creature from the food lagoon pulled itself out of the recycling bin, squelched out of the café and stomped past the giant T Rex skeleton. Its hair was matted with half-chewed grapes and strands of spaghetti, its pinstriped

suit was stained with sour apple juice and gooey
chocolate marks, its shoes were splattered with
soggy crisps and bits of squashed bananas.

'AAAAARRRRRGGGGGHHHH!' roared
the creature.

Mash and Zainab looked at each other with
huge eyes and issued the only instruction that
fitted the situation.

'RUN!' they both yelled.

They raced off with their entire class sprinting behind them. The hideous creature chased after them, howling, 'MY REPUTATION IS SECOND TO NONE!' As the creature ran it threw bits of rotten food off its clothes.

'FOLLOW US!' yelled Mash, as he and Zainab zoomed up a flight of stairs. The class followed but the creature was gaining on them. At the top of the stairs was a long corridor. To the left a burly security guard, having heard the creature's screams, was running towards them.

'THIS WAY!' shouted Mash and Zainab, making a sharp right and pelting forward. The class were now being pursued by the creature *and* the security guard. At the end of the corridor a second security guard appeared and lunged for Zainab and Mash. They swerved round his outstretched arms and he went sprawling on to the floor. The other children jumped over him and ran on.

'NO CHILD HAS EVER GOT THE BETTER OF ME!' screeched the food-bin creature.

Mash and Zainab sped through an archway and into another gallery. The class piled in after them, but everyone suddenly froze. This wasn't like the other galleries in the museum – they all had an *entrance* and a *separate exit*. This gallery had just one door – it was the entrance *and* the exit. A second later, the creature and FIVE security guards burst in.

'This isn't good,' said Zainab.

'There's nowhere to run now!' seethed the Mr Sharpish creature, pulling some egg-fried rice off his nose in an attempt to look less like an alien and more like a stupendously furious supply teacher. 'I told you – no children have EVER got the better of me!'

'I think you might find this useful,' said a sixth security guard, entering the room and handing Mr Sharpish a disk.

'What is it?' he demanded, pulling a mouldy blueberry out of his ear.

'It's the CCTV pictures of that monster chap meddling with the power dial of the Earthquake Simulator.'

'BRAVO!' shrieked Mr Sharpish, flicking a mouldy apple core off his shoulder and eyeing the disk affectionately. 'Does it have any other footage?'

'It will have loads of them running round the museum like a gang of out-of-control trouble-makers,' nodded the guard.

'Excellent!' grinned Mr Sharpish, licking his lips and spitting out a piece of squidgy apple core.

He turned to face the class. 'I can't WAIT to get back to school and show this disk to Mrs Makepeace. Finally, she will get to see the true nature of Mr Armoury's DISGRACEFUL CLASS!'

'We can't let her see that disk,' hissed Zainab,

'or we'll be in trouble for the next year and they'll probably send you home.'

'I know,' agreed Mash, 'but what can we do?'

'Leave it with me,' replied Zainab, her hand shooting up in the air. 'Er, Mr Sharpish,' she said humbly. 'Can Mash and I go and get the trolley where we left our lunch boxes?'

'If you must,' snapped Mr Sharpish, cradling the disk like a newborn chick, 'but hurry up. We need to get back to school for Mrs Makepeace's little horror show!'

Mash and Zainab ran out, Zainab explaining her plan on the way. But it wasn't to the lunch room they headed. They jolted to a halt outside the security guards' room. It was empty because all of the guards were with Mr Sharpish and the rest of the class. Zainab minded the door while Mash crept inside to carry out Zainab's genius plan. They then quickly scooted off to get the lunch box trolley.

*

On the train back to school, everyone was in a very glum mood, except for Mr Sharpish, Mash and Zainab. First Mash taught Zainab how to push a peanut along the carriage floor with her nose; then Zainab taught Mash how to moonwalk.

This is cool, thought Mash, *although it's a bit hard on the toes!*

He practised up and down the aisle, at one point barging into Mr Sharpish.

'WATCH WHERE YOU'RE GOING, YOU OAF!!' shouted Mr Sharpish, pulling a strand of spinach off his eyebrow and glaring furiously at Mash. But Mash moonwalked happily back to Zainab.

Mr Sharpish managed to tidy himself up, and the second they arrived back at school he ordered the class straight into the music room, where a large TV was situated. He dispatched Danny Nolan to go and get the head teacher.

'What can I do for you, Mr Sharpish?' asked

Mrs Makepeace when she arrived.

'It's more like what I can do for *you!*' simpered Mr Sharpish, inserting a disk into the DVD player. 'You are about to see the true nature of Mr Armoury's class – a group of students who are INCAPABLE of completing any task, who tampered with a high-voltage piece of equipment, and ran through a magnificent museum like a HERD OF WILDEBEEST!'

Mrs Makepeace looked stunned.

Mr Sharpish pressed play on the DVD player.

An image of the class working diligently in the rivers and oceans section of the museum appeared on screen. This cut to them studiously taking notes by the dinosaur collection. Mr Sharpish muttered something under his breath and quickly skipped to the next scene. This portrayed the children writing copiously about lower spotted Mandrogal plants, Roman fish farming, and the bones of loose-jawed elderly crocodiles, in addition to composing letters

to Inca tribesmen.

'I like your joke about them being incapable of doing any work!' beamed Mrs Makepeace. 'I DO see the true nature of Mr Armoury's class. It's wonderful you appreciate how dedicated to learning they are!'

'NO, NO, NO!' blurted out Mr Sharpish. 'Those aren't the right bits!'

He furiously spooled forward again and this time a picture appeared of him squelching around the museum, totally covered in food waste.

Everyone burst out laughing.

'And how WONDERFUL of you for getting into the spirit of things, Mr Sharpish!' beamed Mrs Makepeace. 'Mr Armoury *would* approve!' She turned to face the class. 'Children, you will be receiving a certificate of commendation for your first-class behaviour and the excellent work you completed on the trip. WELL DONE!'

'B ... b ... but,' spluttered Mr Sharpish, 'you haven't seen the—'

'I've seen plenty, thank you, but now I need to return to my paperwork. Well done, Mr Sharpish, for sharing all of this outstanding work with me!'

And with that, she exited the room briskly.

Mr Sharpish faced the class with a wild look in his eyes, his cheeks, nose and lips twitching with near hysteria.

I'LL GET YOU FOR THIS!

he screamed.

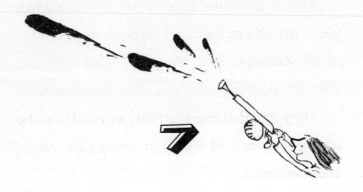

7

'How did you do it?' asked the rest of the class in the playground after school.

'Before we got the lunch box trolley we ran to the security guards' office,' explained Mash. 'I used my laser eyes to burn a new disk containing bits of us all working really hard and Mr Sharpish as the squelch monster.'

'And then on the train coming back, when Mash was moonwalking up the carriage, he bumped into Mr Sharpish and switched the discs!' added Zainab.

'Genius!' cried everyone, slapping Mash and

Zainab on their shoulders.

That night after supper, Mash and Zainab were in Zainab's room playing mini-cricket when Zainab's dad came in. 'That was Mr Sharpish on the phone again,' he announced.

They stared at him fearfully, worried that the supply teacher had told him about their antics at the museum.

'He wanted permission to take you on *another* school trip tomorrow,' explained Zainab's dad. 'I know it's unusual to have two trips in succession, but I said yes.'

They waited until Mr Kaur had left the room and then Mash said, 'He will *so* want revenge.'

'Maybe he'll take us to a medieval dungeon, lock us up and throw away the key,' said Zainab.

*

But when they got to school the next morning, instead of a look of hatred and revenge on his face, Mr Sharpish was smiling broadly while ushering everyone on to a coach. When they were all on board he stood up at the front.

'Children,' he began, 'I've been wrong about you and wrong about Mr Armoury.'

The class gaped at him in shock.

'He is obviously a fine teacher who has taught you very well.'

'Are you joking?' called out Mash.

'Absolutely not,' replied Mr Sharpish. 'I thought long and hard about everything last night and the truth is you *did* get the better of me at the museum. I mean, come on, I was squelching around as a food-waste beastie!'

He started chuckling. Some of the children joined in with his laughter.

Mash narrowed his eyes.

It is so weird to see that man smile. I don't trust him one tiny bit!

'And as a way of apologizing for being so unkind to you, I'm taking you on a very special trip today – somewhere FUN!' said the now-grinning teacher.

The coach pulled away and, rather than telling everyone to be quiet on the journey, Mr Sharpish strolled up and down the aisle, chatting to people, laughing and even singing (very badly) when the driver flicked the radio on. A short while later the coach drove past some massive gates bearing the sign: PAYBACK TV STUDIOS.

'Are we going to watch a TV show being made?' asked Zainab.

'We're going one better than that,' smiled Mr Sharpish, 'we're going to be *on* a TV show, or more specifically, *Trash the Teacher!*'

There was a massive cry of delight from the class.

'YESSSS!' shouted Zainab. 'It's one of my favourite shows!' She grinned at Mash. 'You get to humiliate your teacher! All of Payback TV's shows are about kids getting their own back on adults!'

Mash frowned. 'Hang on a minute,' he

called out to Mr Sharpish. 'What about your reputation? Won't it be ruined if you go on a show like that?'

'Forget my reputation!' replied Mr Sharpish. 'It's time I loosened up!'

Everyone cheered, piled off the coach and ran inside the building. Massive photos of the TV station's stars were plastered all over the walls in Reception. A man in a smart black jacket with a name badge stating 'Bob' sat behind a long chrome desk. Mr Sharpish had a quick chat with Bob and then a woman with tightly packed ash-blonde hair appeared. She was wearing an earphone/microphone combo and a badge labelled 'Suzette'.

She led them down several corridors before announcing, 'Welcome to the Green Room.'

'But this room isn't green,' said Mash as they filed inside. There were several plush beige velvet sofas and paintings of multicoloured custard pies on the walls.

'It's just a posh name for a waiting room,' explained Suzette in her unusually high and shrill voice. 'It's where guests relax before they appear on a show, and eat of course.'

The class turned round and saw a long table piled high with biscuits, cake, crisps and cartons of juice. As Suzette left, they fell on the goodies like a swarm of locusts and within minutes the table was completely bare.

'Mr Sharpish, can I go to the toilet?' asked Zainab after the mini feast.

'OK, but be quick,' he grinned. 'We're on very soon. Your opportunity to show me up, big-time, is about to happen!'

'Come on, Mash,' said Zainab.

'I can't believe everyone's fooled by him smiling a bit,' said Mash as they hurried out of the Green Room.

'You think it's all an act?' asked Zainab.

'Definitely!' replied Mash firmly. 'The guy's a fraud!'

'But he's about to be on *Trash the Teacher*. He must know what he's letting himself in for.'

Mash huffed. 'I still don't believe him,' he muttered darkly.

There were no signs outside the Green Room, but after traipsing down numerous corridors they finally located the ladies' toilets. Zainab ran in while Mash waited outside. After she emerged, they walked back the way they *thought* they'd come, but after a number of turns, the Green Room wasn't anywhere in sight.

'We're lost,' said Zainab, horrified at the prospect of missing out on their possibly-once-in-a-lifetime TV appearance.

They pressed on and were starting to get desperate when they saw a man in baggy jeans and a long-sleeved baseball T-shirt striding towards them. He was carrying a clipboard and wearing a name badge stating 'Brian'.

'Er ... excuse me,' said Zainab, hurrying up to him, 'but we need to get back to the Green Room pronto.'

'Which school are you from?' asked Brian.

'Willow Street Primary,' replied Zainab. 'We're on *Trash the Teacher*.'

Brian studied his clipboard and shook his head. 'Your school *is* on a show,' he replied, 'but it's not *Trash the Teacher*.'

'I don't understand,' said Zainab.

'Ambleford Primary School are on *Trash the Teacher*,' he explained. 'They're a bit late but they just phoned to say they're nearly here.'

'So what show *are* we on?' asked Mash.

Brian checked his clipboard again. 'Willow Street Primary are on *The Pupil Punisher*.'

'The *what?*' cried Zainab in alarm.

'It's a brand-new show,' explained Brian. 'As all of our programmes are about kids embarrassing grown-ups, we thought it was time for grown-ups to get some of their own back on kids. *The Pupil Punisher* will enable a teacher to totally humiliate his class. It's going to be fantastic. You're the first class to ever be on it.'

Zainab's mouth dropped so far open that her bottom lip could have tied her shoelaces.

I knew it! thought Mash triumphantly.

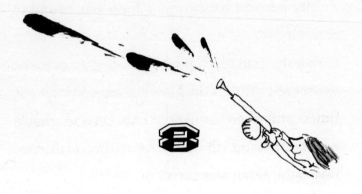

'I can't believe I trusted him,' groaned Zainab, but Mash's mind was already working furiously on what they could do with this new information.

'Brian,' he said, 'Where are the two shows being filmed?'

'*The Pupil Punisher* is in Studio 1. *Trash the Teacher* is in Studio 2.'

'And where are those studios in relation to the Green Room?'

Brian consulted his clipboard again. 'Studio 1 is a three-minute walk from the Green Room.

Studio 2 is just on the other side of the Green Room, but you have to go a long way round to reach it.'

Mash pulled Zainab to one side and whispered an idea to her. She nodded several times and then grinned. The second they'd finished talking, she pointed at the small two-way radio Brian was carrying.

'Can you contact the Green Room with that thing?' she enquired.

'Yes,' said Brian.

'Could we borrow it to get a vital message to our teacher, please?'

Brian flicked a switch and handed it over to Zainab, who passed it on to Mash.

'Er … it's a private call,' said Mash.

Brian sighed, squashed his clipboard under his arm and put his fingers in his ears.

Zainab and Mash pressed their ears against the receiver.

'Hello!' said a voice from the Green Room.

'Mr Sharpish?' asked Mash, speaking in a very low voice.

'Yes.'

'This is … Bob … from Reception.'

'How can I help you, Bob?'

'I need to see you about the upcoming, televised final of the *Teaching Reputation of the Year Award*. You've been nominated for the prize.'

'Really?' said Mr Sharpish with delight. 'At last my genius has been recognized! But can I see you *after* the show we're on? It's being filmed very soon.'

'Unfortunately it has to be now,' replied

Mash, 'but don't worry, it'll only take a minute.'

'OK,' agreed Mr Sharpish, 'I'll race down to Reception right now.'

Mash handed the radio back to Brian, who withdrew his fingers from his ears.

'Could you tell us the way to Reception, please?' asked Zainab.

'I thought you wanted the Green Room,' said Brian with confusion.

'Slight change of plan,' cut in Mash.

Brian flicked through the sheaves of paper on his clipboard and produced two floor plans of the building. 'Take these,' he said.

'Thanks!' shouted Mash and Zainab, running off down the corridor, maps in hand.

Thirty seconds later they skidded to a halt outside Reception. They hid behind a large plant pot, pushed the door open a tiny fraction and peeked in. Mr Sharpish had just arrived, out of breath after a mad dash from the Green Room.

'You told me to report here?' he said breathlessly.

'Excuse me?' said Bob, from behind the chrome desk.

'About my nomination for the *Teaching Reputation of the Year Award*?'

Bob looked blank.

Mr Sharpish was about to pursue his enquiry further when the doors from the street were flung open and a very harassed-looking female teacher, with short grey hair and large round glasses, burst into Reception, her class flying in after her.

'Mrs Custler, Ambleford Primary School!' she panted. 'I phoned to say we were running late.'

'Er, Bob?' said Mr Sharpish.

But Bob ignored him and addressed Mrs Custler. 'I'll get Suzette to take you straight down to the studio,' he said, reaching for a phone.

'I'm just out here,' called an unseen Mash through the door, in a high and shrill voice that sounded very much like Suzette's.

'Thanks, Suzette,' called Bob, indicating for Mrs Custler and her class to go through the doors.

The Ambleford party hurried in the direction of Mash's voice.

'You keep Mr Sharpish here for a bit longer,' Mash hissed at Zainab. 'I'll deal with Ambleford Primary and see you back in the Green Room.'

'Cool!' nodded Zainab.

So as the Ambleford party pushed through the door, Zainab went the other way to intercept Mr Sharpish.

Mash smiled warmly at Mrs Custler and her party. 'I'm Suzette,' he declared. 'This way please, Ambleford!'

Mrs Custler looked up at Mash. 'Is it dressing-up day or something?' she enquired.

'It's for Monsters In Need,' replied Mash.

'Oh,' said Mrs Custler, reaching into her purse and dropping several coins into Mash's left ear.

Mash checked his map and led the Ambleford party briskly down a corridor. A few minutes later, he pushed open the door of Studio 1.

'I think this is the wrong place,' said Mrs Custler as she saw the set with the words THE PUPIL PUNISHER splashed across it in giant letters.

'They told me you were a man, Mrs Sharpish, but never mind,' said the show's producer – a tall, bespectacled woman called Natasha – striding over to Mrs Custler.

'Er ... I'm not Mrs *Sharpish* and this isn't the show we're supposed to be on, so could we just ...'

'Too late to back out now, Mrs Sharpish!' laughed Natasha, slapping the hapless teacher on the back.

'Enjoy the show!' called Mash shrilly, racing

out of the studio, checking his map, and haring back to the Green Room. He was delighted to discover that Zainab and Mr Sharpish weren't back yet.

'What's going on?' asked the rest of the class.

'We're going to make a grand entrance!' he laughed.

It's time for a bit of Flamby architecture!

Mash blinked five times and two fiery red beams shot out from his eye sockets. He used these to cut a perfect door-shaped hole in the wall. With the help of Carly, Eddie and Danny Nolan he dragged the cut-out section of plaster and concrete and hid it behind one of the velvety beige Green Room sofas. They'd just finished this task when Zainab and Mr Sharpish hurried in.

'We're on!' called out Mash, pointing to the new opening.

'I didn't notice that door before,' frowned Mr Sharpish.

'These TV people are so clever with their designs, aren't they,' nodded Mash, 'but we need to go through NOW!'

He ushered Mr Sharpish and Zainab through the gap, with the rest of the class following. They found themselves in a backstage area, covered with large black curtains.

'How did THEY get in here?' asked a man carrying a microphone.

'Who cares?' replied a woman dressed as a nuclear warhead, making a beeline for Mr Sharpish.

'I'm Annabel Anarchist, presenter of *Trash the Teacher*,' the woman explained. 'They told me you were a woman, Mr Custler, but never mind!'

She turned the tip of her warhead towards the class. 'Kids – you go through and load yourselves up.'

The children raced through the black curtains.

'Er, I think there's been a mistake,' said Mr Sharpish.

'I understand your nerves, Mr Custler,' said Annabel, grinning reassuringly, 'but we need to press on!'

Two beefy men suddenly appeared at her side.

'Get this one trussed up!' she instructed.

The men picked Mr Sharpish up and carried him through the black curtains on to the stage.

'What's going on?' he enquired anxiously as the bright studio lights hit him.

A second later, he was lowered into a tiny

orange vehicle and strapped in with two tight metallic straps.

'ROLL THE CAMERAS!' bellowed an offstage voice.

'WAIT!' shouted Mr Sharpish hoarsely. 'This is all wrong. I shall have to ...'

But a button was pressed on the side of his vehicle and a second later, it shot forward at **_phenomenal speed_**.

The orange Gungemobile raced round the curved narrow track above the studio audience and screeched to a halt at its highest point.

'OK, Mr Custler!' shouted Annabel. 'Here's Question Number 1.'

Mr Sharpish was babbling with rage and trying to protest, but Annabel Anarchist ignored him. 'If Robert lives next door to Keisha, Harry lives two doors down from Sebastian, and Omar lives at the end of Hannah's road, what colour is Gary's football?'

'W ... w ... what?' spluttered Mr Sharpish.

'I'm afraid I can't repeat the question,' said Annabel.

'Er ... purple?' volunteered Mr Sharpish.

'YOU FAIL!' shrieked Annabel, pulling down hard on a purple lever. The Gungemobile zoomed down the slope at breakneck pace. Every member of Mr Armoury's class hoisted up the gunge guns they'd been given, and fired blobs of shiny red goo at the teacher trapped inside.

'THIS IS AN OUTRAGE!' yelled Mr Sharpish, getting more and more plastered with goo, but his voice was drowned out by the screams and laughter of the class and the baying audience.

'IT'S TIME FOR THE PLANK 'N' PLUNGE!' hollered Annabel, dancing up and down on the spot and encouraging the audience to scream even louder.

A giant metal hand swung over, undid the

metal straps of the Gungemobile, lifted Mr Sharpish up by his head and dumped him on to a plank jutting out from a fake pirate ship. The 'water' below consisted of a frothing mass of freezing, mushy peas.

'If seven equals four and three equals nineteen,' bellowed Annabel, 'what's the square root of one thousand, three hundred and sixty-seven point five?'

'Er ...' Mr Sharpish began frantically counting on his fingers.

'I'LL HAVE TO HURRY YOU!' screeched Annabel.

'Er ...'

'YOU FAIL!' shrieked Annabel deliriously.

She flicked a switch and the plank swung down, tipping Mr Sharpish into the icy green depths, while the class fired more red gunge at him. From the depths of the mush a huge boot suddenly swung up, kicking Mr Sharpish into the air and sending him into a giant baby's crib which was filled with soggy rusks. Long plastic feelers placed a giant nappy round him, stuck a baby's bonnet on his head, and a dummy in his mouth.

'What is the capital of the Burra Dip Islands?' shouted Annabel. 'Toe City, Vase Village or Flag town?'

'Er ... Flag Town,' said Mr Sharpish after spitting the dummy out.

'The Burra Dip Islands don't exist!' screeched Annabel. 'ONCE AGAIN – YOU FAIL!'

She twisted a dial and a grabber lifted him out of the crib and threw him into a large whirlpool bath. He was spun round and drenched in hot soapy water, which cleaned off all of the mushy peas, rusks and goo. An instant later the bath's 'Ejector Plug' threw him out of the bath. He crashed across the studio floor, landing on a barber's chair, where a massive drier fanned the hapless teacher dry.

'CONGRATULATIONS FOR FAILING

SO APALLINGLY IN FRONT OF OUR STUDIO AUDIENCE!' beamed Annabel, whacking Mr Sharpish on the back. 'Do you have a message for the nation after being COMPLETELY HUMILIATED?'

She shoved a microphone in his face.

'I ... I ... I ...'

'AND CUT!' shouted a voice.

Mr Sharpish stood there spluttering for a few moments and then, with incandescent rage, he leapt out of the barber's chair and screamed, 'WHERE IS THE SHOW'S PRODUCER? I DEMAND TO SEE THEM THIS INSTANT!'

A thin man with a goatee beard, a tweed jacket and name badge stating 'Marcus Hebden – Producer' walked over to greet him.

'THIS PROGRAMME CAN NEVER GO OUT ON TV!' bellowed Mr Sharpish, waving a spindly finger at Marcus. '**NEVER, EVER, EVER!!!**'

'Erm ... it actually just went out live,' replied Marcus.

'Live?' repeated Mr Sharpish in a strangled whisper.

'Live,' Marcus nodded.

For a second Mr Sharpish stood frozen to the spot like a particularly shocked and furious ice sculpture, and then he turned on his heels and raced out of the studio screaming. His scream was so loud that everyone in the studio heard it, everyone in the building heard it and everyone within a three-mile radius heard it.

And the two words he repeatedly screamed were:

'MY REPUTATION!!!'

Mash and the rest of the class went absolutely ballistic – cheering, whooping and jumping up and down on the studio floor. But Zainab's voice cut through the crescendo of noise.

'QUIET, EVERYONE!' she shouted as a sobering fact clunked into her brain.

It took a few moments, but everyone eventually fell silent.

'What's the matter?' asked Eddie. 'We got rid of him, didn't we?'

'Yes,' replied Zainab, 'but if you haven't noticed it's only *Wednesday* and Mr Armoury isn't back till next *Monday*. As soon as Mrs Makepeace discovers we've got rid of Mr Sharpish, we'll be mincemeat.'

'Zainab's right!' nodded Mash.

'We need to find another teacher, and quick,' said Zainab.

She and Mash led everyone quickly through Mash's makeshift Green Room door and back towards Reception.

'We're stuffed,' whispered Zainab.

But the second they arrived in Reception, the door swung open and in walked ... Mr Armoury!

10

The class stared at Mr Armoury in total shock.

Mr Armoury looked back at them with even more shock.

Then all thirty kids plus Mash raced towards him, shrieking with joy.

'All right, all right!' he laughed, fending them off. 'Everyone come outside and let's work out what's going on!'

There was a patch of grass outside Reception and when everyone was sitting down, Mr Armoury faced Mash. 'I'm so sorry I wasn't here to greet you on Monday, Mash. It's excellent to finally meet you. How's your time in human school going?'

'It just got a zillion times better,' grinned Mash.

'That's great,' said Mr Armoury. 'Now can someone tell me what on earth you are all doing here?'

'You go first,' said Zainab. 'Why are you back from your course and what are you doing at the TV studio?'

'I got a call telling me I'd been nominated for the *Teaching Reputation of the Year Award*,' explained Mr Armoury, 'and as the course ... er ... finished early, I came straight here to talk about it. What about you lot?'

'Mr Sharpish got us on *Trash the Teacher*,' replied Zainab.

'It was awesome!' grinned Mash. 'We really splattered him!'

'Where *is* Mr Sharpish?' asked Mr Armoury.

There was silence for a few moments and then everyone started shouting at once.

'He was awful!' cried Eddie.

'Dreadful!' moaned Robbie.

'Appalling!' exclaimed Carly.

'Oh no,' said Mr Armoury quietly, 'you didn't scare him off, did you?'

Everyone suddenly looked very guilty, apart from Mash. He'd just spotted a piece of paper that had fallen out of Mr Armoury's rucksack on to the grass. He reached out with the knitting needles section of his trunk and pulled it towards him. Lifting it up, he read it quickly. He tugged Zainab's elbow and showed it to her. As she read her eyes grew larger.

'Look,' sighed Mr Armoury, 'whatever you may think of someone, you can't just hound them out. I'm afraid I'll have to tell Mrs Makepeace about this.'

'Of course,' piped up Zainab, 'but if you talk to her about that, we'll just have to show her this.'

She held up the piece of paper.

'What's that?' asked Danny Nolan.

'It's a series of notes between Mr Armoury and another teacher called Mr Sutton,' explained Mash. 'They were on the Hattie Practice course together.'

'That's right,' chipped in Zainab. 'Let me share these notes with everyone. Remember, they're about the course that finished *early*.'

Mr Armoury went very red in the face. 'Er …

I don't … think … that … is …' he spluttered,
but Zainab had already started reading.

Dear Mr Sutton – This course is <u>so</u> boring!
If I have to listen to Hattie Practice for
one more second, I'll eat my notepad.

Mash took over.

Dear Mr Armoury – I couldn't agree
more. It's dire, rubbish, garbage – the
absolute pits.

Zainab picked it up.

Dear Mr Sutton – If I have to stay here
till Friday I'm frightened my ears will fall
off. I'm going to sneak out after breakfast
on Wednesday and not come back. I'll tell
my head teacher that the course finished
early.

Mash read the last one.

Dear Mr Armoury – Brilliant idea! I'm going to do the same. There are so many of us here, she won't notice that two of us have left. Soon we'll be free – YAY!!!

Mr Armoury's mouth opened, closed, and opened again.

'If you agree not to speak to Mrs Makepeace about us and Mr Sharpish,' said Zainab, 'this piece of paper will miraculously get destroyed.'

'That's … that's blackmail,' spluttered Mr Armoury.

'No,' grinned Mash, 'that's justice!'

'I think you just got the better of me,' admitted Mr Armoury, trying not to show his admiration for Mash and Zainab's negotiating skills.

Mrs Makepeace was watering a flower basket at the front of the school when the coach returned.

'Mr Armoury,' she said in surprise, 'what are *you* doing here?'

'He completed the course before everyone else,' declared Zainab. 'He was so good, he was allowed to leave early, isn't that right, Mr Armoury?'

'No ... I mean ... yes,' said Mr Armoury, 'absolutely! I ... I was given permission.'

'Well done,' nodded the head teacher, 'but where is Mr Sharpish?'

'He had terrible earache,' replied Mash. 'His reputation for hearing is second to none, so he went to have his ears checked out.'

Mrs Makepeace pursed her lips, and for a minute it looked as if she didn't believe this story, but then her mobile rang and she stepped a short distance away to take the call. Mr Armoury and the class stood waiting for her.

'That went well, didn't it?' grinned Mash.

Mr Armoury smiled weakly.

They watched as Mrs Makepeace ended the call then dialled a number to hold another quick conversation.

A few moments later she was back with them. 'Wonderful news!' she beamed. 'That was Hattie Practice on the phone. She told me she was very sorry to lose you early, Mr Armoury, but says she has another course coming up very soon. This one is for *two* weeks and it's in the middle of nowhere, so no one will be able to leave early! I've just booked you a place on it!'

Mr Armoury looked completely shell-shocked.

'And I have superb news for you too, children. I've just found another brilliant supply teacher to stand in while Mr Armoury is away.'

Looks of horror spread through the class.

'Unfortunately Mr Sharpish can't do it.'

The sighs of relief from the children, particularly Zainab, were so loud it was like a football crowd.

'So I've booked Mr Sharpish's older brother,' beamed Mrs Makepeace. 'He has a reputation for being much stricter than his younger brother, but I'm told he delivers very challenging and absorbing lessons! Isn't that wonderful?'

Mr Armoury and the class looked at each other in total horror.

NNNNOOOOOOOO!'

they all wailed at the top of their voices.

When danger threatens, call SOS!

This is edge-of-your-seat drama which takes our heroes Michael and Katya all over the planet, fighting to survive natural disasters and protect the natural world.

From a small island in the Philippines, to Baring Island in the Canadian Arctic and the wild savannahs of Africa, these are no ordinary adventures!

Jim Eldridge

Meet Dave. He's disgusting.

Dave wants to know everything about how
things work, and that means getting up close
and personal with really disgusting things!

www.hodderchildrens.co.uk

Hodder
Children's
Books